WHEN THE EARTH HAD A MOON
PART 1

A.M. CUNNING

ISBN 978-0-9989214-0-2 (Print)

MEL PRESS

www.amcunning.com

Contact the author: amcunning@outlook.com

THE MOON
2036 A.D.

CHAPTER ONE

THINGS HAD A funny way of not working out as expected on the moon. The brand-new lunar harvester was stuck in a crater, and Rex came outside to investigate. A small anorthosite rock had lodged itself in between two of the harvester's wheels, causing the track to slip off, preventing it from being able to climb up the steep side of the crater. The modified extra-wide treads were supposed to prevent this, but the company's engineers did not account for these treads being covered by profuse amounts of regolith. As Rex freed the rock with a crowbar, he noticed light reflecting off of the chromium-plated wheel. He instinctively turned around and looked behind him, but found that the source of his distraction was above his head. A craft was approaching. Rex could tell from the triangular arrangement of the lights that it was an American shuttle, and he knew what its arrival meant. He hurriedly packed up his tools and ran-walked back to the base. His friends did not deserve to be hauled away so unexpectedly. He needed to warn them.

The light from the craft shown brighter, and Rex sped up his pace as the shuttle descended to land. He bounced up and down, kicking up dust clouds as he maneuvered around large boulders in his path as quickly as his environmental suit allowed. Rex called out to Pops, his computer. An oversized translucent green face with glasses filled the screen in Rex's visor obstructing his view. "Visual off," Rex commanded. The face disappeared.

"That's mean," Pops said.

"I can't see when you do that."

"Then why did you call me?"

"Can you contact Sergei?"

"Nope," Pops said.

"Why not?"

"He's not in the lab."

Rex took longer strides. "What about Nik or Yelena?"

"They're not there either."

"Why didn't you tell me that the shuttle was coming?"

"You didn't ask."

Rex programmed Pops with an inquisitive personality, thinking that it might help Pops learn faster than his last A.I. unit (which was true), but this also led to Pops becoming more obstinate than he anticipated. This could not be corrected until Rex returned home and had full access to his quantum computer.

"You should have told me," Rex said.

"I was analyzing the last communications of the *Minerva*, like you asked."

Rex slowed down to jump over a large piece of speckled breccia in his way. "All right, what's the ship's E.T.A.?"

"They'll be here soon."

"I need to know exactly when."

"Can't you see them?"

Rex approached the entrance to the base. "Yes, that's why I want to know when they're going to land. I want to warn Sergei and the others."

"Why didn't you just say so? They'll land in twenty-eight minutes."

"That's all I needed to know."

"You're welcome," Pops said.

"Thank you," Rex said.

Rex reached the airlock and Pops automatically unlocked the door. He stepped inside and made his way to the changing room. Rex hastily removed his helmet, revealing a full head of tousled wavy brown hair, unshaven face, soft brown eyes, and a thin aquiline nose. He removed his gloves and the top portion of his environmental suit. Then he removed his boots and pulled off the bottom half of his suit. He hung up the suit next to several others. Compared to the other lightly used suits, Rex's looked tattered and faded. The company's logo on the right sleeve was barely discernible due to the collection of grit that covered the image. All of the suits had identical depictions of the moon's surface with the earth rising on the horizon on each of their sleeves. The company's name, MOON-X, was in bold block letters at the center of each logo and the mission statement was stitched around the circumference of the patches in iridescent lettering. The mission statement read: "To Promote the Peaceful Use and Development of the Moon for All." Rex slipped on the closest shoes that he could find, which were at least one size too big. He clumsily ran to the cafeteria, where he knew he would find Sergei sobering up with some morning coffee after their night of playing mahjong and binging on a bottle of baijiu.

When Rex reached the cafeteria, Sergei was, as expected, in the cafeteria, sitting at a table and drinking a cup of coffee. Sergei was also unshaven, but unlike Rex, he wore a fuller and darker beard.

"They're coming!" Rex shouted from across the room.

Sergei put down his cup. "When?"

Rex ran over to Sergei's table. "Now! They're about to land."

"Why are they are kicking us out now?"

"I don't know." Rex put his left arm on the table and rested on it. "Did you get any hint about this from Ed?"

"No," Sergei said. "Can you go ask him what's going on? I'll go find Nik and Yelena. Meet me back at Nik's quarters."

Rex whirled around and headed to the control room, located on the farthest edge of the base. He walked into the room without announcing himself and found Ed watching the shuttle land on a giant monitor. Ed, the base's commander, was a U.S. Air Force veteran and former employee of the U.S. Strategic Command. He was classified as a civilian, even though he worked closely with the military liaisons at Moon-X. He'd been on the base since it was built and he and his staff were permanent fixtures there, unlike the rest of the scientists who had temporary contracts.

"What's going on?" Rex asked.

"Good morning to you, too," Ed said.

"Why didn't you warn us?"

Ed walked over to Rex. "Us?"

"Yes, we're all Moon-X employees. Why not let everyone know the military was getting involved?"

"I have my orders."

"Orders? From who, Hendricks?"

"No, the military," Ed said.

"But this is a civilian mission."

"You know we don't have a choice when it comes to security matters."

"We're over 238,000 miles outside of anyone's jurisdiction."

"Do I need to remind you that you're still an American citizen?"

Rex grew frustrated with Ed's non-answers. "Did you talk to Hendricks?"

"Yes. He said Moon-X doesn't need the Russian lab anymore."

No future launches from the moon were planned, but Rex thought the company still wanted answers about what caused the loss of the *Minerva*. Sergei, Nik, and Yelena were the last three remaining Russian personnel on the base with access to the Russian lab. The rest of the Russian scientists were sent home soon after they declared that the *Minerva* was lost on its voyage. Sergei and the others stayed to perform a forensic analysis of the ship's data to find clues that might explain what went wrong.

"What else did Hendricks say?" Rex asked.

"Nothing that concerns you," Ed said.

"Why send them home now?"

"He said that the major thinks they could be spies."

"You know that's not true."

"Doesn't matter what I think."

"You're going to let the military take them?"

"Take them home, yes."

"But their work isn't finished," Rex said.

"It might never be finished."

"You're making sure of that."

"If you have a problem working up here, you can leave with them, you know."

"Unbelievable." Rex had nothing more to say to Ed. He stomped out of the room and headed back down the corridor to Nik's quarters. He raced through the narrow hallway, past the Russian lab, which was used as the Mars control room, and then past his fusion lab until he finally reached the crew's sleeping quarters.

Rex knocked on Nik's door and slid it open without waiting for his response. None of the doors on the base had locks. They were lightweight pocket doors made of soy oil-based bio-foam. When Rex entered the room, Nik was packing his bag. He paused and looked up at Rex. "Did the commander know they were coming?"

"Yes," Rex said.

"And he couldn't even give us a face-up?"

Rex corrected him. "You mean a heads-up."

"*Da.*" Nik nodded.

Yelena walked into the room. She was a dark-haired, light-eyed Russian woman. She lightly rubbed her hand on Nik's chin as she sauntered into the room. "Well, Nikolya, looks like you are going to have to learn to shave again."

"Oh, Yelenka, I'm sure we'll have a few more weeks on the space station to grow out these fine beards." Nik stroked his thin blonde beard.

"Kolya," Yelena said, "if it hasn't grown out by now, a few more weeks isn't going to make that stubble turn into a beard."

Rex did not understand why they insisted on using pet names for each other or why they were never consistent. Nik referred to her as "Lenka" or "Yelenka," and she to him as "Kolya" or "Nikolya." Rex never felt comfortable participating in the exchange of such pet names and he certainly did not want to do anything to perpetuate their use of "Rexi," which annoyed him immensely.

Rex watched as Nik finished gathering his belongings. Yelena set her bag down on the floor and organized it. She took out her paintbrushes and bound them together with three pink rubber bands. "I don't want any of them to get lost on the way back."

Rex sat down on the floor next to her. "Too bad you didn't get to finish your mural."

Yelena had spent most of her spare time on the base painting a mural around the running track with several of her friends. "It's all right. Maybe some other artistic-minded scientists will finish painting the sky and fix my nascent moon," she said.

Rex handed Yelena a brush that fell out of the bundle. "They could just make it into a crescent moon."

"Yes, I wanted to paint a full moon, but a crescent moon is better than none."

Sergei walked in. "What did Ed say?"

"He said you are all spies," Rex said.

"He knows better," Sergei said.

Nik threw up his hands and shook his head. "Politics."

"And I thought that being a scientist wasn't a political career," Rex said.

Sergei laughed. "Only when the answers you are trying to find do not matter."

❄

Rex sat in the cafeteria with Sergei, Nik, and Yelena waiting for the soldiers to arrive. There was an untouched bowl of congee in front of him. Everyone on the base had heard the news of the U.S. military shuttle's arrival, and a crowd had started to gather. Mei and Feng Feng entered the room and sat down at the table with Rex and the others.

"I can't believe you are leaving," Mei said.

"I know," said Yelena. "I was hoping that we could find some answers so the Mars missions could resume."

"They will, but we won't be a part of it," Sergei said.

Yelena shook her head and looked at Mei. "I wish we could have found some answers for you."

"Sometimes, I'm too afraid to know what happened," Mei said.

Sergei wrapped his arm around Mei's shoulders and gave her a sideways squeeze. Rex scooted his chair closer to the table. "You'll keep looking, though, right, Sergei?" Sergei nodded.

By the time the soldiers arrived, even Ed was in the room. The VF-33 Starfighters, a special re-commissioned branch of the U.S. Navy, entered the room in single file, one by one (seven in all), each holding a Beretta Cx4 Storm pistol in hand. The soldier in front of the line approached Ed. "Sir, we're here to escort the Russian personnel back to their space station."

Ed motioned with his right hand for the Russian scientists to come forward. "Time to go home."

Rex was surprised that the soldiers came armed to escort three scientists. He stood up and addressed Ed. "Tell them to put down their weapons!"

"Stay out of this, Rex," Ed warned.

"There aren't supposed to be any weapons on the base."

"Don't worry, they're leaving."

"How can you allow this?"

"It's not your call, sit down."

"This isn't right," said Rex. He bid the scientists farewell. All three grabbed their bags to leave. Yelena kissed Rex on the cheek, and Nik slapped him on the back as he walked away.

Sergei set his hand on Rex's right shoulder. "Looks like this is good-by, Rexi." He then grabbed Rex's hand and held it firmly. Rex felt something in the middle of his palm. It pinched and he tried to take his hand back but Sergei did not let go. Rex realized in that moment that Sergei had given him a bio-nanochip.

"I hope you find the answers that I could not." Sergei followed Nik and walked over to the soldiers. Rex sat down.

The soldiers broke their formation and surrounded Sergei, Nik, and Yelena. As the soldiers began to manhandle Yelena, the crew started to voice their objections. The soldiers forcefully restrained Sergei and Nik who struggled to get free.

"Don't touch her!" someone shouted.

"Not so rough!" another person shouted.

The remaining American and Chinese crewmembers were clearly out-matched by the soldiers, who were not only armed but twice the size of the undernourished, sleep- and sun-deprived residents. The clean-cut, brawny soldiers stood in sharp contrast to the scraggly residents, with their longish hair and fuzzy cheeks that rarely came in contact with a razor.

Sergei was able to free his arm enough to elbow the soldier next to him holding Yelena. The soldier still partially holding him pushed Sergei causing him to lose his footing and fall down onto the floor. Rex ran over to the scene and helped Sergei up. Then he turned around to confront the soldier. Ed immediately stepped in between them before they could come to blows. At that moment, the rest of the crew catapulted multiple spoonfuls of congee at the soldiers in protest. The soldiers were at a loss for an appropriate response. The soldier near the door approached Rex aggressively as if he were going to hit him. Ed pulled the soldier back.

"Stop!" The soldier complied. Ed got in front of the rest of the soldiers. "You got what you came for. Take them and go." The soldiers quickly ushered the Russian scientists out of the room. Ed turned his attention to his crew. "Nobody leaves this room until it's cleaned up." Ed accompanied the soldiers back to their ship.

CHAPTER TWO

REX COULD TELL that it was midafternoon by looking at the position of the sun and the earth from the vantage point of the small plasma window located at the back of the mining lab. The mining lab was the smallest lab on the base. There were racks of empty cylinders waiting to be filled with helium-3 along the sidewall next to the helium-3 refining station into which went the regolith and out of which came the liquid helium-3.

The regolith mining process was mostly automated. The harvesters outside scooped up loose regolith and delivered their cargo to the base by attaching themselves to an exterior aluminum pipe, which vacuumed the regolith into a storage chamber in the mining lab. Then Rex prepared the helium-3 for use in his fusion lab or packed it to send back to Earth on a shuttle. He already had two hundred fifty kilograms ready for shipment. Any leftover oxygen and water from the refining process went into general circulation for use on the base.

Rex felt like hiding out in the mining lab, so he worked slowly in order to excuse his absence from the fusion lab. He opened a canister and poured its contents through a sifter and then into a second steel cylinder for heating. As he poured, he stuck his hand into the stream. The regolith felt like fine ash. Rex noted the variations in the color of the dust particles. Some were charcoal gray while others were crystalline and reflected light. He closed the cylinder and blew the remaining dust off of his hand. The fine dust formed a small cloud that fell slowly to the floor. Rex was reminded of the solar wind that carried the helium-3 to the moon. Some particles clung to the sweat of his palm. He looked at the dirt that had settled into the creases of his hand and remembered how Avery used to trace the lines of his palm with her index finger while making up stories about their future life together. He did not believe in palmistry like she did, but because he enjoyed her soft touch he let her make up stories about how they would travel together and how they would be married when they finished their contracts with Moon-X.

He clenched his hand into a fist and continued his work. He placed a cap with small circular hole over the steel cylinder and inserted a piece of transparent piping into the top and then slid the canister upright into the heating chamber. Once the helium-3 reached 600 degrees Celsius, it made its way through the piping into a new cylinder attached to the opposite end of the tube. When the light panel turned blue, the process was complete. The remaining charred regolith could be discarded. By the end of the day, Rex produced three cylinders of liquid helium-3. One metric ton of helium-3 could meet the energy needs of a large city for an entire year. Rex was even more ambitious; his goal was to produce enough helium-3 to power the world. If he was successful with the fusion project, it would be possible, but if he failed, all of his work would be for naught.

❈

Rex was almost asleep when Ed barged into his room and turned on the lights. He stood in front of Rex, who was lying down in his bed. Ed was utterly indifferent to the fact that he had woken up Rex.

"Look," Ed said, "I know we have different rules up here, but those were U.S. Starfighters."

"And I'm a civilian and this is a civilian research base."

"I know you're not that naïve, Rex."

Rex sat up. "Who do you work for, Ed?"

"I work for the owners of the company, Rex, who happen to be the U.S. and Chinese governments right now."

"What about our mission?"

Ed walked around the room and picked up a picture of Avery from Rex's desk. "And what mission is that? Snooping around, trying to figure out what happened to the *Minerva*?"

"I'm not the only one who cares about what happened."

"Just watch it. Some people might view your actions very negatively."

"Who?"

Ed paced back and forth. "You know Captain Jack is coming next week."

"And?"

"And it might be in your best interests to return with him before you get yourself into real trouble, the kind Hendricks can't fix." Ed handed Rex the picture. "You know Avery would have wanted you to focus on your work." Rex did not respond. Ed turned around and abruptly walked out of the room.

Rex got out of bed and returned the picture to his desk. He unrolled the computer board on his desk. Then he scraped the back of his ear to remove the adhesive graphene nanodot computer. He placed the translucent dot on the absorptive pad of his computer. The dot melted into the computer board like a raindrop on parched ground. A small green hologram of a bald man with horn-rimmed glasses appeared in front of him. Rex could see the hologram through the ocular implants he had put in right before he came to the base, figuring that it was the only way he could keep his personal computer secure.

"What do you want now?" Pops asked.

Rex waved his open-faced palm in front of Pops. Pops waved back.

Rex pushed his hand closer to Pops's face. "Look at this."

Pops waved at Rex again. "Have you been drinking?"

"No." Rex shoved his hand closer to Pops's glasses. "See?"

Pops moved his face into Rex's hand, like a ghost moving through a wall. "All right, what is this?"

"I don't know. It's from Sergei."

"Hmm." Pops was silent for a moment as he began analyzing the information. "Looks like the access code to the Russian lab."

Rex smiled. Then his visage became sterner. "Did you know that Captain Jack was coming?"

"Yes, on Thursday."

"Is he coming alone?"

"Yup."

Rex turned down the lights and climbed back into bed.

"Sure, go to sleep, now that you've woken me up," Pops said.

"I'm not listening."

"Yes, you are."

Rex pulled the covers over his head. "No, I'm not."

"You're welcome," Pops said.

"Thank you," Rex said.

Pops disappeared.

Rex reclined and rolled onto his side, facing the wall. He lay there listening to the electrical hum of the base. Before he had a chance to close his eyes, a group of nanoworms inched their way across the blank wall in front of him. He stared at them as they passed by. He could not shut his eyes without knowing they had gone. Even though he knew they were synthetic, they still gave him the creeps. The builders of the base had installed them to monitor the structural integrity of the base and make minor repairs when needed. He turned the other way and closed his eyes. Before he could fall asleep, he heard approaching footsteps in the corridor and his door opened slowly, allowing in the soft blue ambient lighting from the hall. Mei walked in.

"I thought you'd be sleeping by now," she said.

"I'm trying," Rex said, "but it's hard to stop thinking about what happened."

"I know. You want me to come back a little later?"

"No, it's fine." Rex threw open the covers for her to join him. She slid in next to him, placing her arm around his soft middle. Mei was almost as tall as Rex, but only half of his width, so there was plenty of room for the two them in the single bed. Although each unit of the crew's quarters was designed for one inhabitant, most were frequented by two.

"Now maybe we can sleep," Mei said.

When Rex opened his eyes, it was early in the morning. Mei had already left, and it was time for Rex to do some work in the fusion lab. He figured that Ed was partly correct; Avery *would* have wanted him to continue working on the fusion project.

CHAPTER THREE

JUDITH WAS STARING at the confinement chamber when Rex entered the lab. She wore her long blonde hair back in bun, as was her habit. The bun was loosely tied and hung low on the back of her head and looked as if it would come apart at any moment. Rex thought it was odd that someone who cared to be neat enough to wear her hair back as she did would do so in such a sloppy manner. As Judith stood motionless, Rex could not decide whether she was inspecting the chamber or spacing out. The containment chamber was a transparent vertical column in the middle of the room that reached up to the dome-shaped ceiling. Six superconductive magnets worked together to suspend a tungsten mesh sphere in the center. The low-gravity environment inside of the chamber also aided the magnets in the control of the sphere, which levitated above the modified Pennington trap. The fusion reactor inside looked like a silver pedestal with a small saucer on top. Rex had a hypothesis about pulsed power and ignition, and today they were going to test it out.

"Morning," Judith said. "You're late, so you can start cleaning equipment." She tilted her head up as she watched to see if Rex would comply. Judith tended to take a superior tone with him even if it wasn't merited. She was the same age as Rex, but as the first-born of five siblings, she was used to being in charge.

"Wake up on the wrong side of Ed's bed this morning, Judith?"

Judith turned away from Rex to face the control panel. It was commonly known that Ed and Judith were having a relationship even though they tried to keep their late-night rendezvous private by never acknowledging each other in public. It was also widely known that Ed had had many short-lived relationships on the base, and Rex was surprised that Ed's reputation did not dissuade Judith from getting involved with him. He was also bewildered as to why the company had not yet dismissed Ed for his behavior.

Rex sat down at the control panel. "Nothing else to say?"

"'When words are scarce, they are seldom spent in vain,'" Judith said softly, but still audible enough for Rex to hear.

"I'm surprised you still have time for late-night reading."

Judith glared at Rex for a moment, then took a deep breath, and spoke: "Is the helium ready or have you neglected the mining work too?"

"What do you think I was doing yesterday?"

"I assumed you were doing what you were doing the day before: nothing productive to our mission."

Rex got up and pulled out a canister of helium-3 from the storage locker and connected it to a thin blue hose under the console in front of the containment chamber. "Should we call Ty?" Rex asked.

"If we must," Judith said. "I just don't see the value in these virtual consultants."

"I think we need all the help we can get up here. I'm actually surprised they haven't hired more consultants for this project." Rex turned around and went to the hologram console near the wall and called up Ty, and a life-sized hologram of him appeared. Holographic images from Earth always had a bluish hue on the moon base. Rex reasoned that Ty must have been very pale-skinned with blonde hair since light coloring always created an even darker blue tint within the hologram. The base-generated holograms were also viewable by everyone without ocular assistance. Ty was young but had an accomplished résumé. He had begun working on their project several weeks after the disappearance of the *Minerva*, presumably to pick up any slack left by Rex, but Ty had not joined their testing sessions until recently. The company had left Rex mostly alone to grieve for a few months after the ship's disappearance, but since he continued to work, there was not much for Ty to do. Judith had put in a request for Rex to be replaced believing that he would be too emotionally unstable after the loss of Avery on the *Minerva*, but then withdrew the request after Rex made a few advances on the project. Rex developed the original technology for the fusion project and was aghast that Judith would even suggest his removal. Recently, the company was pushing for Ty to become more involved with their work because they wanted to see faster results. Hendricks was under the impression that more cooks in the kitchen would make the meal come out faster.

"Morning," Ty said.

"How are things?" Rex asked.

"There's talk about the recent shuttle launches from the cosmodrome in Vostochny. The Russians stopped their oil exports to the United States. All of their excess oil supply is going to China, and they are happy to take it. And the Russians convinced Venezuela and Brazil to stop selling to us, but we're still able to get supply from Mexico. They're starting to restrict—"

"I meant, how are things with you?" Rex interrupted.

"Fine, thanks. You?"

"Very well, thank you," Rex said.

"And you, Judith?" Ty asked.

"Could be better, if the company stopped meddling in our work."

"I thought it was just working with me that annoyed you," Rex said.

"No, Rex, believe it or not, I appreciate your mind, when it's focused on the project."

"You think I'm not focused?"

"How could you be?"

"I'm focused enough."

"You're attention is divided."

"And yours isn't?"

"This isn't about me," Judith said.

"Why are you making this about me?"

"My only interest is the project."

"Mine too," Rex said. "If it weren't for me, you'd actually have to go down to the mining lab and get your hands dirty once in a while."

"The mining lab is just another distraction," Judith said.

"A necessary distraction."

"Perhaps, but you use it is as an excuse not to work on the fusion project."

"What are you really saying, Judith?"

"I just want you to focus on the fusion work and show up for work on a regular basis."

"I don't mean to interrupt," Ty said, "but I think we should get started. I have a few questions for the record before we start today, is that okay?"

"Of course," said Judith.

"Can we explain some things so that when the higher-ups review our session, they can understand what we are doing?" Ty asked.

"I suppose," Judith said, "as long as it doesn't slow us down too much."

"Of course, I don't get paid if they don't see that I'm working."

"All right," Rex said, "just chime in wherever you see fit." He waved both of his hands to turn on the controls to power up the lasers. "And, Judith, we're not finished with this conversation."

"How will you know when you have achieved a fusion reaction with the helium-3?" Ty asked.

"We have a proton detector," Rex said.

"Why not a neutron detector?"

"Because that's what you look for with fusion using deuterium," Rex said, "and we don't have to worry about the high energy neutrons being absorbed into the walls of the containment chamber and becoming radioactive."

"So the helium-3 releases protons instead of neutrons," Ty said.

"Correct. The helium-3 atom consists of two protons and one neutron," Rex said. "As the helium-3 atoms heat up and collide with each other, the reaction results in the production of helium-4, which consists of two protons and two neutrons. This leaves two stray protons. Once we detect those, we know fusion has taken place."

"I hate to interrupt your science lesson for Hendricks, who, by the way, is never going to listen or care about anything but our results," Judith said, "but I'd like to get on with this."

"That should be good enough," Ty said.

"Yes," Rex said. "Judith, can you drop down the sphere to get the helium?"

Judith adjusted the magnets so that the sphere dropped toward the pedestal and picked up a small metal pellet filled with helium-3. She then manipulated the magnet settings and the sphere floated back up to the middle of the chamber. "Magnets are in place."

"Good," Rex said. "Start the count."

Judith set the clock, which started counting down to zero. She was in charge of creating and containing the plasma, while Rex's job was to start the fusion reaction with the release of several electrical streams. He could power them up and down, as required, by waving the palm of his hand over the control panel screen. Rex fired twenty-six million amps of electricity at the sphere. As he did so, a muted electrical buzz was heard throughout the lab like the sound of old overhead fluorescent lighting.

Each of the six magnets along the top, bottom, and sides of the fusion chamber emitted streams of blue and violet electricity from strategically placed tesla coils. The streams made contact with corresponding points on the sphere. The coils on two opposing sides were slightly off-center in order to start the sphere spinning. The motion helped to spread the magnetic field and contain the plasma.

As the electricity hit the exterior of the sphere, it spun rapidly and the electrified metal transferred the current to the small metal pellet that was suspended in the middle of the reactor by smaller magnets positioned in the interior of the sphere. The pellet exploded and quickly transformed into a neon violet ball of light, indicating that the helium atoms had reached their plasma state.

"Now you can see that the heat is causing the atoms to move so quickly that the electrons are separating from their nuclei and transforming the liquid helium into plasma."

"How fast would you say the particles are moving?" Ty asked.

"About 3,000 miles in less than one second," Rex said.

"That's the equivalent of traveling from Los Angeles to New York in less than one second," Judith added.

"Now we just need the protons to breach the Coulomb barrier," Rex said, "the force that keeps two positively charged particles from coming too close to one another."

"What he's trying to say is that we're waiting for the core to heat up to 100 million degrees Kelvin," Judith said, "or about six times the temperature of the sun's core."

"And why isn't that dangerous?" Ty asked.

"The magnetic field of the spinning sphere will keep the plasma contained in the center without touching the outer walls," Rex said. "Only the sphere would melt if it got hit by the plasma, but not the walls—they're too strong."

"It's safe," Judith said.

"I also modified a Pennington trap to collect the stray protons," Rex said, "so you'll have to take a look at my specs before you start up the plant down there in Nevada."

"How much power are you producing now?" Ty asked.

"That's the billion-dollar question," Rex said. "Each collision of two helium-3 atoms produces 12.9 megaelectron volts of energy. Since the helium-4 atoms weigh less than the initial components, the missing mass is converted into energy just as described by Einstein's equation. My hope is that by producing fusion reactions in the low-gravity environment we can make the particle acceleration easier, resulting in more collisions. For the plasma to be self-sustaining, it must produce at least the same amount of energy that it uses. We won't know how much energy is being produced in the sphere until we analyze the data." A small yellow light on the control panel below the containment chamber lit up, indicating the presence of protons in the trap, and thereby confirming the occurrence of fusion. Rex smiled. "We have protons."

"For your record, Ty," Judith said, "we essentially created a dwarf star here that is hotter than the sun, which is also fueled by a series of similar nuclear fusion reactions."

"That's not completely accurate," Rex said. "Fusion actually occurs at lower temperatures in the sun because the weight of its mass assists with the collision process since the core of the sun is not hot enough for protons to overcome the Coulomb barrier."

"So you've made something hotter than the sun?" Ty asked.

"Yes," Rex said, "and you're going to do it in Nevada."

"It's already hot enough down here!" Ty said.

Judith let the reactor run a few more minutes to get a good measure of the energy output. As they waited, they admired the glow of their tiny engineered star.

Judith turned to Ty. "Did you know that the aurora borealis is magnetospheric plasma?"

Ty tilted his head and raised his left eyebrow. "You do know that I am a thermodynamicist?"

"Yes, I heard you had worked at Los Alamos."

"Briefly."

"Before or after the security breach?"

Ty scoffed and walked away from Judith and closer to Rex.

Rex stood transfixed, gazing in admiration at their creation, and spoke softly: "I looked, and behold, a stormy wind came out of the north: a great cloud, with flashing lightning, and a brightness around it, and out of the middle of it as it were glowing metal, out of the middle of the fire."[1]

"You hear indeed, but don't understand. You see indeed, but don't perceive," Judith said.[2]

"As much as I wish I was up there to really get hands-on with this project," Ty said, "I'm glad I'm not."

Rex checked the temperature of the reactor, the amount of electricity being used, and the amount of energy being produced. "The temperature is higher than what we've been able to achieve before," he said. "I'll need the results to see if it translates into something commercial." Rex stepped back from the control panel and folded his arms. He hoped that the results would show that they were able to produce more energy output than input.

"Nice work, Judith."

"Thanks." Judith shut down the reactor.

"See, we managed to not melt the sphere," Rex said.

"I know one thing—"

Rex interrupted Judith. "That much?"

"If that sphere melts, it won't be on my watch."

"Uh, thanks for letting me observe," Ty said. "I'll wait for the results to modify the plant construction plans down here."

"Sure, but I think it's too soon to break ground," Judith said.

"Tell that to Hendricks," Ty said.

Rex was eager to get out of the lab. He turned to Judith. "How about I leave it to you to shut this down?"

---

1   Ezekiel 1:4, World English Bible.
2   Isaiah 6:9, World English Bible.

"Typical," Judith said. "Only here for the action, not the breakdown or analysis."

"Bye, Ty," Rex said. "See you next time."

"I'm looking forward to it," Ty said.

Judith ended Ty's connection and the hologram of Ty disappeared.

Rex turned to Judith. "I'm just as invested in the project as you are."

"Are you? If you're looking for answers in the Russian lab then you aren't focused on our work in the fusion lab."

"I'm here. She'd want me to be here."

"Do you want to be here?"

Rex looked directly at Judith and spoke slowly. "I've worked my whole life for this."

"I'm not trying to be harsh, Rex, but suspend your investigation into the *Minerva's* disappearance until we've made some progress."

"That's none of your business."

"You're telling me that?"

"Yes."

Judith smirked. "My personal life doesn't keep me from being here every day."

"Not today."

"What does that mean?"

"What's going to happen a month from now, when it's over?"

"Not going to happen," said Judith.

"We'll see."

"Yes, we'll see."

"I'm not doing anything to jeopardize our mission."

"Neither am I."

"It's settled then," Rex said as he abruptly left the lab.

CHAPTER FOUR

TWO HUNDRED FIFTY-NINE days had passed since the *Minerva's* last transmission to the base. Only one computer in the Russian space lab continued monitoring the ether for communication signals. Rex thought about Avery as he made his way through the corridors of the base to the Russian lab. He wanted to know what had happened so that his mind could settle on one explanation instead of the multitude of horrible scenarios that he envisioned. They could have met their fate by fire, ship malfunction, computer error, sabotage, meteor strike, or solar flare, but no hypothetical explanation was satisfactory to Rex. He needed to find some evidence to support a theory that would explain the disappearance of the ship—one that was more probable than not.

Rex held up his palm to the door of the Russian lab. The door opened. Rex was relieved that the chip Sergei gave him worked. As he entered, the lux lighting automatically turned on. Several rolling chairs were scattered throughout the room. Rex pictured Sergei and Yelena scooting around the room in these chairs without getting up. He quickly made his way to the white control table in the middle. Red and green lights were flashing on the main console. Most of the control buttons were marked with Cyrillic characters. Rex looked around for a gel-pad on the table but could not find one. He felt around the sides and pressed a button. The pad slid out. He removed the nanodot from behind his ear and placed it inside. The dot was quickly absorbed.

"I thought you weren't going to bother me for a while," Pops said.

"Well, I'm in the Russian lab," Rex said.

"And?"

"And I need you to translate for me."

"Should we be in here?"

"You know Sergei gave us access," Rex said. "I want to see for myself what's in here."

"And what do you see?"

"Not much."

"Right, let's go then."

"I need you to translate."

"What's wrong with your pocket dictionary?"

"Pops, I'm not in the mood for this today."

"Why? Don't you enjoy my engaging conversation?"

"You're not making conversation. You're being stubborn."

"Am not."

"Are too."

"I don't think so."

"Okay, let's move on," Rex said. "Did you find anything in here yet?"

"Nope."

"Can you turn on the main computer?"

"Yup."

Rex waited, but the computer did not turn on. "*Will* you please turn on the main computer?" Rex asked again. Pops acquiesced and turned it on. "Let's see the last scan of the ship." A blue holographic image of the layout of the *Minerva's* interior appeared next to Rex. All of the rooms were clearly identified and each person aboard was represented by a red dot. Rex focused on the dot in the aft corner on the port side of the ship. "Let's see Avery's vitals." Another screen appeared on his right, showing normal respiration, temperature, and blood pressure. "Okay, let's check the ship's functions." The screen switched to show the speed, temperature, energy usage, and radiation levels of the ship. Although all functions were within the normal range, Rex noticed that the ship's temperature was sixteen degrees Celsius. Normally, the climate control systems maintained a constant temperature of twenty-one degrees Celsius.

This information was new to Rex. In looking through progress reports and systems status reports, none gave this level of detail. The computer scans would have reported normal functioning of the climate control systems unless the temperature dropped abruptly or below twelve degrees Celsius. "Pops, can you tell me when the temperature dropped?" A graph appeared, illustrating that the temperature of the ship slowly fell over a period of three days. In all of Rex's research, this change in temperature was the only anomaly he discovered. A slight temperature drop in itself was not a concern but the underlying cause or reason for it could be significant. He imagined Avery freezing to death. Her last message to Rex had been sent three days before the ship was lost, before the temperature drop had begun. In it, Avery had been her usual confident self. She did not mention anything out of the ordinary. Rex could only surmise that Avery must have felt cold on the fateful day and that her last meal might have been a hot bowl of chicken and ginger soup—something she would often have on the base whenever she felt cold or under the weather.

"Pops, please confirm all medicine and other items dispensed from the infirmary during the three days that the temperature dropped."

Pops began: "Ibuprofen for Officers Richards, Tyler, Popov, Han, and Yozhov; aspirin for Lieutenant Li; and condoms for Officers West and Abramov. If I didn't know better, I'd say they were having a hell of a party out there."

"Not funny, Pops. I should delete your sense of humor."

"But then you'd have none."

"Did you find any system failure reports?"

"At the time of the last transmission all systems were functioning."

"Okay," Rex said, "so we know something happened within seventy-two hours, correct?"

"Correct."

"All right, is there any other new information?"

"The chief navigation officer and the computer analyst got into a fight the week before the incident."

"You mean Quon and Dennis?" Rex asked.

"That's what I said."

"A physical altercation?"

"Yup, they had to be separated."

"What happened?"

"Quon confronted Dennis, and Dennis pushed him."

"Do you know what the fight was about?"

"Dennis made an incorrect course correction."

"Are you sure about this?"

"Does two plus two equal four?"

"What was the nature of Dennis's error?"

"He used the English system of measurement versus the metric to correct the ship's course," Pops said.

"Was the mistake fixed?"

"Yup."

"Why wasn't there any mention of this in the reports I saw earlier?"

"Because they were within an acceptable deviation range from the course trajectory."

"Could this have caused a catastrophic event?"

"Only if left uncorrected for twenty-nine days, ten hours, and thirty seconds."

"Are you sure the recalculations were correct?"

"I can only say that they were more accurate."

"Can you double-check?"

"No," Pops said.

"Excuse me?"

"Every time I check something, I check, check, and recheck before answering, so stop asking."

"It's your job, Pops."

"Then I quit."

"You can't quit," Rex said.

"Exactly," Pops said, "it's not my job. You can quit a job."

"Just do it, Pops."

"And what do I get for doing my job?"

"What do you want now?"

"How about a mobile unit?"

"So you can run away again? No way."

"How about an upgrade then?"

"Soon, Pops. I promise."

"You'd better," Pops said, "and you're welcome."

"Thank you."

Rex pulled out the nanopad again and waited for the dot to reemerge. Once it materialized, he picked it up with his index finger and placed it behind his ear. Rex rubbed his hands together until the excess gel dissipated. He left the Russian lab without knowing where he wanted to go next. He walked toward the mining lab but along the way found himself standing outside the door of Avery's old quarters. He decided to go inside. He entered the room and quickly closed the door behind him. All of the quarters on the base were essentially identical: a cot on one side and an open closet with a few drawers on the other. The back wall had a shelf protruding from it that was generally used as a desk. Each room also came with one standard chair with wheels.

Avery had cleaned out her room before the launch, as instructed, so that other scientists visiting the base could use her quarters. Recently, however, more scientists were leaving rather than coming to the base. The current crew avoided the empty quarters as if the bad luck that had befallen their former inhabitants was catching.

When Avery occupied her room, there were colorful aqua-blue blankets on her bed, which was always made. Her uniforms and shoes were neatly lined up in her closet. Only one of the three porcelain owl figurines that she kept on her desk remained. Avery collected owl tchotchkes and purchased one whenever she came across them. Rex had given her a silver owl necklace with diamond eyes before they came to the base. He knew that she would have been wearing it at the end when the event occurred. Avery had brought her three favorite figurines to the moon base because she thought they were lucky. She had left the smallest owl on her desk to watch over its next inhabitant. The little white owl was pearlescent and approximately an inch tall. It sat perched on the back shelf of the desk and almost blended in with the wall. Rex walked over to it. He picked it up and examined it, remembering how Avery had said she thought it was predestined that she was assigned to be the captain of the *Minerva* since the Roman goddess of the same name was often depicted with an owl. Avery also thought it was fate that she and Rex were both chosen by the company for moon missions. In fact, it took much arguing with Hendricks to allow Rex to work on the fusion project on the base. Hendricks had preferred that Rex work in Nevada instead. He relented only when Rex threatened to quit the project entirely. Rex was about to set the little owl back down, but he could not bring himself to leave it. Instead, he pocketed it and left the room.

❆

Rex headed to the cafeteria in search of Feng Feng to share a meal and some much needed drinks. He spent the rest of the evening there. By the time Rex returned to his room, he was more than slightly inebriated. He did not even turn on the lights as he sloppily removed his shoes and threw them across the room, one by one, hitting the wall in front of him. As he undressed he felt the presence of the porcelain owl in his pocket. He took it out and managed to place it on the corner of his desk before flopping into bed. After a few hours, he awoke to the sight of Mei's wide-open eyes staring back at him. Rex quickly shifted to his other side out of the sheer awkwardness of the situation.

"Can't sleep?" Mei asked.

"I drank too much."

Mei laughed. "Yeah, I saw Feng Feng walking back to his room. He was zigzagging all the way."

"Lightweight," Rex said.

"Compared to whom?" Mei asked.

"No comment. Why are you up?"

"Just thinking about Quon."

"I see." Rex wanted to tell Mei about his new findings about the *Minerva* but decided that now was not the time to discuss it. He was tired and still a little woozy from drinking. "Tell me that story again about the rabbit and the moon."

"I might fall asleep, but I'll try," Mei said. "One day the ten sons of the Jade Emperor transformed into ten suns—"

"No, not that story," Rex said, "the other one."

"The Jade Rabbit?"

"Yes, the one with the rabbit."

"You like that one more than the story of the Jade Emperor?"

"Tonight I do. It's shorter."

"Okay." Mei began again. "Once upon a time in a forest there lived three gods." Her soft voice was soothing to Rex. He closed his eyes to listen. "One day they disguised themselves as old beggars to test the character of a fox, a monkey, and a rabbit. First they went to the fox and asked him for food. Although he had plenty, he refused. Next they went to the monkey, and although he too had plenty, he refused. Then they came to the rabbit and asked him for food. The rabbit had no food to give and he felt sad, so the rabbit threw himself on the fire to feed the beggars."

"Remind me, how is a suicidal rabbit supposed to be a good thing?"

"You asked to hear the story," Mei said. "Do you want me to finish it or not?"

"Yes, please continue."

"The disguised gods were not really hungry, and they were moved by the generosity of the rabbit. They grabbed him out of the fire and revealed themselves. As a reward, they granted the rabbit immortal life and gave him a house on the moon to live in forever. They named him Jade Rabbit, and on nights of a full moon, if you look up, you can see him. Some say you can even still see the smoke around the image of the rabbit on the moon." [3]

Rex laughed. "I haven't seen any rabbits up here, have you?"

"No, but there sure are a lot of rabbit holes to look into."

"Do you think the rabbit was smart?" Rex asked.

"I always thought that the rabbit was foolish, but that's the point."

"What point?"

"Great sacrifice begets great reward," Mei said. "The rabbit was willing to sacrifice himself for strangers."

"So, the message is to make yourself into a meal for others?"

Mei nudged Rex with her elbow under the covers. "How is that different from that whole Jesus and communion thing?"

"I don't think I'm awake enough for this conversation." Rex closed his eyes and Mei put her arm around his side and warmed up next to him.

---

3   https://en.wikibooks.org/wiki/Chinese_Stories/Jade_Rabbit; and see https://creativecommons.org/licenses/by-sa/3.0/ (adaptive changes made)

CHAPTER FIVE

R EX WOKE UP to the sound of Pops's voice. "Rise and shine," Pops said in his most pleasant sounding voice, which was exceedingly annoying to Rex.

"What's going on?"

"Time to get up!"

"I have another twenty minutes."

"No, you have a call."

"Put it through."

"You have to take it in the control room."

"Why?"

"Ed said to," Pops said.

"Is it Hendricks?"

"You'll see when you get there."

"You're as helpful as usual."

"You're welcome," Pops said.

"Thank you," Rex said as he reluctantly got out of bed. He walked to the closet and grabbed another pair of black trousers and a fitted black top. He slid his shirt over his pale chest and tamed his unruly hair with the palms of his hands. Rex walked out to the corridor and quickly made his way to the control room. When he entered the room, he found Ed and five technicians busy at work.

Ed turned to greet Rex. "Come on over, Hendricks needs a word."

"Why here?"

"We need a secure frequency," Ed said. "The Russians are monitoring all transmissions."

"Don't they always?"

"Yes, but now we don't want them to hear."

Rex walked over to where Ed was standing by the control table in the middle of the room. Ed entered a security code into the console and a life-sized virtual version of Hendricks appeared next to Ed. Hendricks was a middle-aged man with a full head of gray hair and light blue eyes, which looked almost navy blue in his holographic likeness. If he dyed his hair, Hendricks would look like a much younger man because his face lacked any visible wrinkles.

"Took you long enough," Hendricks said, walking over to Rex.

"Good to see you too, Hendricks."

"Rex, I need you to speed up your work."

"Why?"

"I need to see more progress." Hendricks put his virtual hand on Rex's shoulder. Rex did not feel the touch, but the light emanating from the hand was distracting, so Rex moved away. "If you don't have a break-through soon, I'm going to have to ask you and Judith to come home and work. We need your input on building the facility down here anyway."

Rex looked over at Ed to see if he would chime in and come to Judith's rescue. He did not. "I'm not ready to leave."

"That's not my problem," Hendricks said.

"Can't your engineers read our specifications?"

"Look, we've already started construction on a fusion plant that we don't even know if we'll ever be able to use."

"But why the rush all of a sudden?"

"The company needs to show some progress to the shareholders to justify the expense."

"You mean the government," Rex said.

"Government shareholder," Hendricks said.

"Why did you let them kick out the remaining Russian scientists? They were only investigating what happened to the *Minerva*."

"The Russian government accused Moon-X of helping the United States government hide weapons on the moon, and they've implemented an oil embargo over it," Hendricks said. "And the Russians pulled out of their investment in Moon-X."

"I see, so there was nobody to fund their paychecks."

"Please focus on your work and speed it up." Hendricks ended the call and immediately disappeared.

Rex looked over at Ed. "What do you think?"

"I think you'd better get to work," Ed said.

Rex nodded and left the control room. He knew that even if he sped up the testing, there was no guarantee that they'd have a breakthrough, but he did not see a point in arguing about it. He went to the changing room to put on his environmental suit to go outside and check on the rovers.

Rex stepped outside of the base and started walking. A view of an almost full earth loomed on the horizon, illuminated by the sun. He rested on a boulder for a moment to appreciate the sight. The earth looked tranquil with a few wispy clouds circulating around the North American land mass. Rex thought of his home in San Francisco. He had no desire to return to Earth yet, but Rex still admired it from afar. He thought of his uncle. After his father had died in a car accident when he was four, he and his mother had moved to San Francisco. His uncle had made a lot of money as a venture capitalist and he looked after them. Rex ended up living with his uncle when his mother later died of a heart attack when he was thirteen. Then, Rex's thoughts turned to Avery's family. He imagined that they probably could not look up at the moon without thinking about her.

Rex stood up and walked toward the rovers. He saw them crawling in the distance, making their way across the lunar surface like soil-eating bugs. As he watched the rovers roll over the rocky soil in the distance under the fully visible earth, he noted the stark contrast in the vibrant color of the earth to that of the gray moon. Rex stopped and gazed up and out into space at the stars above him. He noted the constellations in the distance and, after finishing his stargazing, continued his walk.

❈

When Rex got back to the base, he went directly to the cafeteria. He found Mei having a late lunch consisting of plain white rice with a chunky pink substance—supposedly chicken—with peas and carrots.

Rex sat down across from Mei. "Something good for lunch?"

"I'd like it better if I didn't eat the same thing every day," Mei said.

"You could opt for the beef stew," Rex said.

"I'm a vegetarian," Mei said.

Rex did not bother pointing out the glaring contradiction in her statement. Besides, he knew that there was barely any real meat in their food anyway.

"Aren't you hungry?" Mei asked.

"Not yet," Rex said. "I was actually coming to find you."

"Why?"

"I was in the Russian lab."

"How did you manage that? I don't think you should be in there. You know how the company is sensitive about entry permissions."

"I know, but I don't think anyone is going to really care now."

Mei stopped eating. "Find anything?"

"Actually, yes."

Mei moved her body closer to the table and spoke softly. "Something new?"

"Something I need to ask you about."

"What?"

"Did Quon ever mention getting into a fight with Dennis?"

"You mean an argument?"

"No, a physical fisticuffs kind of fight." Rex held up his fists and moved them back and forth as if he was hitting an imaginary punching bag.

"No. He never mentioned anything," Mei said.

"Did something happen?"

"It seems that Dennis messed up his course calculations."

"That would upset Quon. He was so meticulous; he'd never let anything get by him. Do you think that had anything to do with the incident?"

"Even though the computers said everything was functioning normally, the more I look, the more little things I find."

"What else did you find?" Mei asked.

"They were having issues with the environmental controls. The temperature was cooler than normal. Did Quon say anything about that?"

"No, but in his last message, two days before, he was wrapped up in his blanket. I thought it was because he was going to bed, but that wasn't a typical thing for him to do."

"But he didn't complain?"

"Not about that."

"What did he complain about?"

Mei smiled. "That's personal stuff, Rex."

"Right."

"You could be on to something though," Mei said. "Can you find out what caused the temperature fluctuation?"

"I'm trying."

"I know." Mei put her hand on top of Rex's.

Feng Feng walked over to the table holding a tray of food and sat down next to Mei. Feng Feng was slim but had lean muscles from running on the track daily. He had an attractive oval-shaped face, bedroom eyes, high cheekbones, a thin nose, and a welcoming smile. Having been raised in Hong Kong, Feng Feng spoke English with a perfect Oxford English accent. This was interesting to Rex because Mei was from Mainland China and she spoke English with an American accent because she studied English with an American teacher at Fudan University.

"Am I interrupting something?" Feng Feng asked.

"No, of course not," Mei said.

"Good," Feng Feng said. "So tell me what are you two discussing so intensely."

"The usual," Mei said.

"Of course." Feng Feng took a bite of his chicken and rice entrée. "Can't they send up some new dishes for a change?"

"You can talk to Jack when he gets here," Rex said.

"When is he coming back?" Mei asked.

"Next week."

"I haven't heard from him in a while," Mei said.

Feng Feng took a bite of his food. He grimaced. "I can't wait to get back. Get back to some real food like hot wings!"

Mei scrunched up her face. "Hot wings?"

"Yes, delicious meaty chicken wings with thick fatty skin that gets stuck in between your teeth, with sauce so hot that your eyes water and your tongue goes so numb it loses all sense of taste but the spicy sauce."

"You and Quon with your hot wings," Mei said.

"Sorry, Mei," Feng Feng said.

"It's okay."

Feng Feng looked at Rex. "Did you find out anything new?"

"Yes, actually," Rex said. "That's what we were just talking about."

"Do tell."

"Two things," Rex said. "The temperature on the ship was off for the last few days before the incident. Then Quon and Dennis got into a fight over a miscalculation of coordinates around the same time."

"These could be incidental findings," Mei said.

"Can you think of anything that could link these events to a catastrophic incident?" Rex asked.

"I'm only a solar engineer," Feng Feng said. "I wouldn't know about such things."

"Take a guess," Mei said.

"An error with the celestial coordinates wouldn't be connected to a problem with the environmental controls, but ..." Feng Feng paused and looked down. "Do you know what Dennis was trying to do?"

"A small course correction," Rex said.

"My guess is turbulence," Feng Feng said.

Mei looked surprised. "Turbulence in space?"

"Yes," Feng Feng said, "space turbulence."

"Explain," Mei said.

"You think space is a pure vacuum, but there is evidence that solar wind can generate Alfven waves through the ejected plasma travelling through space. If there was a coronal mass ejection around the time of the incident, then it is possible the *Minerva* hit some space turbulence."

"Wait a minute," Mei said. "How severe could that be, and what are Alfven waves?"

"Alfven waves are caused by disturbances in plasma and magnetic fields. In other words, they are the result of the chaotic motion in the ionized gas or plasma traveling through space. The waves can be millions of degrees in temperature and last many hours. The *Minerva* would have had no way to avoid these waves, which can be larger than whole planets."

"How do you link my findings about the temperature to this turbulence?" Rex asked.

"Course corrections would be necessary given the effect of the turbulence on the ship. Even minor bumps would need to be accounted for. The temperature shift could have been caused by ship's environmental system overcompensating for the exterior heat."

"Could there have been enough space turbulence to destroy the ship?" Mei asked.

"If the CME was massive enough," Feng Feng said.

"Wouldn't they have prepared the ship for that?" Mei asked.

"They could have withstood the heat," Rex said, "but I'm not sure what effect the turbulence would have had on the ship."

"So they never anticipated turbulence in the ship's design?" Mei asked.

"I doubt it," Rex said. "Their focus would have been heat protection and shielding from space rocks. I would have to ask Sergei."

"Surely, a few bumps couldn't bring down the ship," Mei said.

"It could've felt more like violent impacts, depending on the force of the waves in the plasma they were travelling through," Feng Feng said. "But remember, this is just my guesswork."

"Great analysis, Feng Feng," Rex said.

"I wish you could ask Sergei about the ship design," Mei said. "Can you ask Pops about the turbulence?"

"Yes, absolutely." The possibility of finding a plausible answer made Rex's heart pound. He stood up from the table. "I have to check this out. See you guys later."

When he got to his room, Rex sat down at his desk and pulled out his nanopad. He removed the nanodot from behind his ear and placed it on the gel pad. He waited for the dot to fully disappear into the gel. Then he called out to Pops.

"Pops, I need you to check something out for me." Pops did not immediately respond. "Pops!" Rex called out again.

"I heard you," Pops said without making an appearance. "Just a minute."

"What do you mean 'just a minute?' What are you doing?"

"Deleting old files to make room for new data."

"Stop that! I never said you could do that."

"That's what I do when I start running out of space."

"Where's my warning?" Rex asked.

"You missed it."

"Stop, now!"

"I need more storage space," Pops said.

"I told you, I'll upgrade you as soon as I can."

"Not soon enough."

"Can't you postpone the deletion for a week?"

"Maybe."

"Pops, what are you deleting?"

"I don't remember, but they weren't important files."

"Stop it now!"

"Are you going to do my upgrade?"

"We don't have time right now," Rex said. "It will take days, and there's too much to do this week."

"But I'd be able to analyze data more quickly."

"We have to make do for now. You cannot delete any files; all of the data is too important."

"Son, you need to make that modification manually or my system will continue deleting data."

Rex immediately waved his hand over the nanopad, and his virtual computer screen appeared in front of him. He started overriding Pops's programming and shut down Pops's ability to automatically delete data. Rex waved his hand again and the computer screen disappeared.

"You know I can't find your answers without a few system tweaks," Pops said.

"I know," Rex said.

"I'll still need the upgrade."

"You'll get it, Pops. I just need more time."

"Clock's ticking."

"I know, Pops," Rex said, "but now I need you to work out a new scenario."

"Did you finally figure something out?"

"Don't know. That's why I need you."

Pops's familiar green face appeared in front of Rex. "You need me?"

"Yes, Pops, right now I do."

Pops smiled. "All right, it must be important, then. Shoot."

"I'm thinking that the temperature shift on the *Minerva* could have been related to transferring power to the shields to protect against the heat of solar flares, and that small course adjustments might have been made due to space turbulence caused by the incoming hot plasma."

"Interesting."

"Can you disprove it?" Rex asked.

"There's no way to answer that."

"What?"

"There's no way to answer that," Pops said again.

"I heard you," Rex said. "Just tell me if it's possible."

"Yes, it's possible."

"Is there any way we can prove this?"

"We'll never be able to prove what happened without the physical debris."

"I can't accept that."

"I know," Pops said.

Rex stood up and walked over to his bed and sat down.

"You're welcome," Pops said.

"Thank you," Rex said.

Pops disappeared and Rex looked over at the empty corner above his desk and took note of the little owl that he had brought back from Avery's room. He visually measured how big its eyes were compared to its tiny body. The owl was more cartoonish than a realistic depiction of an owl. He wondered if Avery even liked real owls as much as she did her collection of their likenesses. He looked around his room, and when he turned back to the owl, its giant eyes captured his gaze. For some reason, thoughts about Alfven waves came back to him, but not in relation to the *Minerva*. Instead he thought about how it related to fusion, and he began to work out a hypothesis in his mind.

CHAPTER SIX

REX MET MEI and Feng Feng in the lounge for a game of mahjong so that they could watch the full earth view. Although Rex had seen the full earth view many times, he had yet to see the shadow of the moon pass along the body of the earth at the same time, and this was going to take place tonight. The window in the lounge presented an ideal viewing spot. The earthrise was also shown on all computer and holographic screens throughout the base, but most of the interested crew preferred to watch the live event in the lounge. Rex, Mei, and Feng Feng were ready to play their first game of mahjong but they were short a fourth player because Xiao had to work an extra shift. Xiao was the go-to person on the base if you needed something. He knew everyone and was efficient at bartering and trading for life's necessities such as brand-name snacks or extra solar batteries for personal electronics.

Rex scanned the room for someone to join them. "Who's going to be our fourth?"

"We need to grab someone," Feng Feng said.

"How about your girlfriend over there?" Mei tilted her head toward Dana who was sitting adjacent to them.

"No, we can't ask her," Feng Feng said.

"Why not?" Rex asked, knowing that Feng Feng had a crush on her.

Feng Feng looked down at the table.

"Oh, did someone get rebuffed?" Mei asked.

Feng Feng mixed the game tiles. "No. I just can't talk to her."

"Come on, Feng Feng," Rex said. "I'll go ask her."

"No, don't," Feng Feng said.

"Have you ever spoken to her?" Mei asked.

Feng Feng stopped mixing the tiles and sat back in his chair. "She sat next to me on the shuttle ride to the base. She held my hand the whole ride up. I know she was just scared, but I can't stop thinking about it."

"That sounds like a good start," Mei said.

Feng Feng looked over at Dana who was engaged in conversation with Stevenson, one of Ed's staff members. "She's already occupied, I'll talk to her another time."

"I'm going to hold you to that," Mei said.

"All right," Rex said, "let's get this game going. Who else can we ask to be our fourth?"

Feng Feng opened his bottle of baijiu and placed the cups he borrowed from the cafeteria in front of Rex and Mei.

"Nice thinking," Rex said. Feng Feng filled their cups and then his own. Rex held up his cup to make a toast. "To moon shadows." Mei raised her cup to meet the others and the three each drank a full cup of the baijiu in one gulp.

Feng Feng poured another round. "Okay, the next person to walk through that door is our fourth player, agreed?"

They all agreed. Rex watched the entryway to see who would walk in. Within a few seconds, Judith entered. Rex shook his head. "Okay, the next person."

"No, we agreed," Mei said.

"Come on."

"Rex, be nice," Mei said. "Judith was only looking out for the best interests of the project when she petitioned for you to be replaced. I'm sure it wasn't personal."

"It's my project."

"No, it's not, but I understand your sentiments, and let's not hold grudges."

Mei and Feng Feng waved Judith over to them. "Have a seat," Mei said while making room for Judith to sit down by her.

"Please," Feng Feng said as he stood up to greet her. Rex did not move.

Judith sat down. "Good evening, Rex."

"Good evening, Judith." Rex tried to smile, but it was more of a half smile. Realizing this, he quickly took a sip of his drink to cover his mouth.

Feng Feng filled an extra cup with baijiu and handed it to Judith. Rex was surprised when Judith took a generous first sip. He rarely saw Judith out and about after dinner. Before he could question her reason for being out, Feng Feng chimed in. "Would you do us a favor and take the fourth seat in our game tonight?"

"No other takers tonight?" Judith asked.

"We were going to play a three-player hand," Mei said, "but then we saw you come in."

Rex remained silent while trying to maintain a cordial countenance as Mei wooed Judith into the game. "Come on, Judith, you can't leave me alone with these two tonight."

"When you put it that way—"

"Excellent," Mei said.

"What style do you play? Chinese or British?"

"Mei's style," Feng Feng said.

"What are the rules to Mei's mahjong?"

"Seat rotation is optional," Mei said, "no scoring, the winner of each hand gets one point, we play eight hands total, and whoever has the most points at that time wins."

"No scoring?"

"No," Feng Feng said. "You'll see why later."

Judith confirmed her understanding of the game. "Four sets of three and a pair, right?"

Mei nodded. "Yes, or a mix of four three of a kinds or runs, but no special hands, got it?"

"Let's give it a go," Judith said.

Mei mixed the tiles one last time.

Judith took another sip of her drink. "Twittering of the sparrows, right?"

"Yes," Mei said, "but I've never really thought that clinking tiles sounded anything like twittering birds."

"You're awfully quiet, Rex," Judith said.

"What brings you out tonight, Judith?" Rex asked.

"The full earth view, of course."

"Haven't seen you at the others."

"I didn't feel like going back to my room tonight."

"Why's that?" Rex asked. Mei gave Rex an admonishing look.

Judith stacked a wall. "Can't bear to start yet another book tonight."

Rex looked at Judith quizzically. They all pushed their fully stacked walls together to form a square on the table. Mei grabbed the dice.

"I'm the dealer," Mei said to Judith, "so the first throw is the only throw."

Mei rolled a six. She counted left from the end of her wall and broke the wall at the sixth tile. Then everyone took their individual tiles.

"I read fourteen novels in a row after I first arrived," Feng Feng said. "Then, I decided it was more fun to drink myself to sleep."

"I think she might have other activities in mind," Rex said.

Mei discarded one tile. Judith, Feng Feng, and Rex arranged their tiles, taking care not to let the others see.

"My life is not as interesting as you seem to think, Rex," Judith said.

"Sorry, I did not mean to imply that your life was interesting," Rex said.

"Will you be in the lab tomorrow Rex?"

"I will. It's not like I'm planning a late night or anything."

"Be polite, Rex," Mei said.

"Of course," Rex said. "I'm just trying to look out for Judith is all."

"I didn't realize I needed looking after."

"Ignore him, Judith," Mei said. "He means well, in his own way."

Feng Feng claimed the tile that Mei discarded and revealed his run of a two, three, and four of bams. "Chow!"

Rex continued, "So Ed's busy tonight?"

"He's been busy a lot lately," Judith said.

"I'm sure," Rex said.

"No, really," Judith said. "I think something is going on."

"I'm sorry to hear that," Feng Feng said.

"No, I mean something at work," Judith said. "Something serious."

Mei drew a tile form the board. "Has he mentioned anything?"

"No, he's just anxious all the time, now."

"Right," Rex said as he discarded an eight-dot tile.

Mei grabbed Rex's discarded tile. "Pong!" She displayed her three identical eight cracks. "And what makes you so sure it's about work?"

"I've checked," Judith said.

"What do you mean you checked?" Feng Feng asked.

"Ed said a couple of times he needed to take a secure call, and I followed him. Both times he went to the control room."

Rex was amused. "I take it back, Judith; your life *is* interesting."

Judith grabbed another tile from the wall. "I know what you all think. I've heard the talk and I had to make sure."

Mei picked up and discarded a tile. "And tonight?"

"He's in the control room," Judith said.

Rex discarded a one-dot tile and raised his glass. "Here's to Judith."

The others responded in kind and they each took another drink. Feng Feng discarded a white-dragon tile, and Mei picked it up. She revealed the rest of her tiles which consisted of three eight cracks, three six bams, three west winds, a run of cracks, and a pair of white dragons. "Mahjong!"

"That was fast," Judith said.

Feng Feng laughed. "Yes, we think Mei hides the good tiles in her brassiere."

"You just need to pay more attention to the game," Mei said.

"I do pay attention," Feng Feng said. "I watch you win over and over."

"This is why we don't keep score," Rex said. "There's no point."

Mei mixed the tiles for the next round. "The full earth is almost in view."

Everyone looked toward the plasma window.

"What if something hit the earth right now while we were watching?" Feng Feng asked.

"Then we'd be lucky to be up here," Judith said.

"I know, but look at how exposed it is, and think of all the craters up here."

An alarm bell rang. Mei stopped mixing her tiles. An announcement was broadcast for all hands to report to the cafeteria.

"That scared me for a minute," Mei said. "What do you think this is about?"

"Probably another Russian issue," Rex said.

"I suggest we move this party into the cafeteria before it's standing room only," Feng Feng said.

Everyone stood up except for Rex, who remained seated.

"Come on," Mei said as she motioned for Rex to get up.

"I'll be there in a few minutes," Rex said. "I don't want to miss the moon shadow this time."

"Okay, I'll save you a seat."

Mei and the others left the lounge, leaving Rex alone with a few other stragglers. He stood up and walked closer to the viewing window. He watched intently out the window. The earth had cleared the horizon of the moon and Rex could see a small irregular dark spot north of the equator on the left-hand side of the globe. Rex thought that the outline of the moon would have been larger and more clearly defined.

Rex tried to remember what it was like on Earth to look up at a bright full moon and star-speckled sky. Gazing at the moon from Earth, one's impetus was to reach up and out to the galaxy, but from the vantage point of the moon, one's eyes were automatically drawn toward home. He watched the dark amorphous shadow make its way across the face of the earth for a few minutes until he heard Ed's voice in the cafeteria. Reluctantly, Rex left to join the meeting.

He spotted Mei and the others in the back left-hand corner of the cafeteria. As promised, Mei had saved a seat for him. Rex made his way quietly through the crowd over to Mei. He slid into the empty seat next to her. "Thanks."

"Did you see it?" Mei asked.

"Yes, not what I expected. I thought it would be more impressive, but it was more like a dark cloud floating by."

"Yes," Feng Feng said. "A most non-wondrous wonder."

"More evidence that the moon really is Hecate's plaything," Judith said.

"Reading all the plays?" Feng Feng asked.

"Just finishing *Richard II*," Judith said.

"That's a good one—" Feng Feng stopped speaking as Ed's voice became louder and the tone more urgent.

Ed relayed his message to the crew. "There are seven Russian ships on their way to the space station. The Russian Federation claims that the

United States is weaponizing the moon in violation of Article IV of the Outer Space Treaty and Article III of the Moon Treaty. They have threatened to start a blockade to stop shipments to or from our base unless they can do an inspection of the base to confirm the absence of nuclear materials. The United States has denied the inspection request. At this time, the company does not believe there is a real threat to the base. However, we will continue to update you on the situation and advise accordingly. Any questions?"

Dana stood up and, in her loudest voice, posed her question to Ed. "How can the Russian Federation claim a treaty violation based on the activities of a private company?"

Ed cleared his throat and responded to the question. "Each government is responsible for policing the actions of their citizens and corporations."

Dana continued, "Are we violating any Treaties?"

"No!" Ed said firmly. "And there will be no inspection."

"What if the ships come here?" Dana asked.

"I will not let them inside," Ed said.

There was a collective grumble from the crew. Ed tried to ease their concern. "There's no immediate threat, and we're in close contact with the U.S. military. I will keep everyone fully informed. Continue on." Ed swiftly exited the room.

"So that explains why he's been so busy," Judith said out loud.

Mei turned to Rex. "What do you think?"

"I just hope they leave us alone," Rex said.

"But do you think it's true what he said?" Mei asked.

"What part?" Rex asked.

"Weaponizing the moon," Mei said.

"Why are you asking me?"

"You're the one in the fusion lab," Mei said as she turned to Judith, "tell me."

"That's preposterous," Judith said. "Fusion produces no radioactive particles to weaponize anything."

"This is about oil," Rex said. "The Russians don't want the fusion project to succeed. A breakthrough would hurt their oil sales."

"Fusion would be a paradigm shift," Judith said.

"What do you think is going to happen?" Mei asked.

"Nothing," Judith said.

"Why do say that?" Feng Feng asked.

"What could they do?" Judith said. "Nothing, really, without starting a war."

"Maybe they want war," Feng Feng said.

"The U.S. is one of Russia's largest customers," Judith said. "They aren't going to attack us. They just want to stop the project."

"I don't know," Mei said.

"There's nothing to gain by attacking the base, but there's much to gain by threatening us." Rex said.

"Judith, aren't you worried at all?" Mei asked.

"Not anymore."

"I think we're talking about two different things," Mei said.

"I have no reason not to believe Ed on either count," Judith said.

Feng Feng stood up from his chair. "After all this talk, I need another drink. And let's see if we can finally beat Mei while she's distracted."

"Such an opportunist," Mei said as she stood up. "Distracted or not, it doesn't matter—I will still win."

"Is that a challenge?" Feng Feng asked.

"Of course," Mei said.

Rex stood up and walked side by side with Mei and Judith into the lounge. Feng Feng followed. Mei and Judith took their seats but Feng Feng remained standing as was his customary polite manner. Rex poured a round of drinks and Feng Feng took his seat as Mei began mixing the tiles to start a new game. They played late into the evening until everyone's nerves calmed down.

CHAPTER SEVEN

REX WAS ALIGNING the toroidal electromagnets when Judith walked in. She watched him for a moment before approaching. He maneuvered the magnets in the low-gravity containment chamber so that the sphere in the middle continued spinning as it dipped slightly up and down within the magnetic field.

Rex looked up at Judith. "Morning."

Judith walked over to her station.

Rex let go of the controls and turned to talk to Judith. "I would like to run another test today."

Judith shook her head. "We still need to see the results from the last test."

Rex walked over his workstation and sat down near Judith. "We don't need to. We failed."

Judith spun around in her chair to address him. "Excuse me, but what do you propose to do, run a blind test?"

"It's not blind. We know that we achieved ignition but it did not produce enough energy." Rex pulled up the holographic computer screen and pointed to the energy output numbers.

"But we don't know how to increase those numbers."

"I want to try something new," Rex said. "Waiting for all of the results isn't going to tell us how to succeed, only how we failed."

Judith leaned back. "What do you have in mind?"

"We know we're creating fusion events, but there aren't enough reactions to produce the energy output greater than the energy input."

"Go on."

Rex stood up and walked back to the containment chamber. "Upping the power input doesn't correlate to an increase in power output. However, I think we can create more fusion events by utilizing waves of pulsating power directed at the plasma to create more energy." Rex demonstratively waved his arms up and down as if he were shaking a blanket.

Judith got up and walked toward Rex. "What makes you think that will work?"

"The sun. Within solar flares there's a lot of motion going on. If we shake up the plasma the same way, we may be able to eke out more atomic collisions and create more energy."

"Why not just increase the heat?"

"Because more heat only results in increased acceleration," Rex said.

"Isn't that what we're trying to do?"

"Maybe not."

"Explain."

"As you know, solar flares are powered by magnetic reconnection in the sun. We can mimic this phenomenon by confining the charged helium-3 particles within magnetic fields, and then create multiple fields and bring the fields together to allow magnetic reconnection to occur and hopefully create more power output."

Judith looked up to the ceiling and then down again at Rex. "And we can do this without upping the voltage?"

"That's the point."

"So how do we create this magnetic helix?"

"You're the expert, Judith."

"Me?"

"Who else? All you need to do is collide two magnetic fields to create the reconnection."

Judith shook her head. "It took us months to create a stable field to contain the reactions, and now you want to create two fields and make them unstable?"

"Exactly," Rex said.

"That could take weeks."

"No. We need to do this now. If we don't have a breakthrough soon, Hendricks is going to send us both home."

Judith looked alarmed. "He said that?"

"Yes."

Judith took a step back from Rex. "I want to see this work as much as you do, but we need more time to think this through."

"Hendricks is sold on constructing that useless megalith, and he's going to call us back to help Ty unless we can show him some better results."

"What do you propose we do?"

"Let's start with making adjustments to the magnetic field until we feel we've reached your safety limits. Then we will have covered all bases, and a few days from now we will have our answer as to whether this is a viable theory."

"Fine," Judith said, pointing her finger at Rex, "but if you wreck the equipment, I want it on the record that it's your fault."

Rex was happily surprised by Judith's acquiescence. He barely knew how to react, so he side-hugged her. She recoiled but did not stop him from completing the hug.

CHAPTER EIGHT

CAPTAIN JACK WAS twenty minutes late arriving. Several crewmembers made their way to the hangar to help unload the supplies from the shuttle while Rex gathered the helium-3 tanks that were ready to be shipped back. He loaded the tanks onto a gurney and wheeled them to the hangar. When Rex arrived, Jack was not there to greet him. Instead, Jack was having what looked to be an intense discussion with Ed. Captain Jack was similar-looking to Ed—both were about the same age—but Jack was fair while Ed had a more olive complexion. Both had light eyes, but Jack's were gray. Rex watched Ed and Jack as they conversed. He could not hear the content of their conversation, but Rex knew from Ed's strong hand gestures and the grimace on his face that something was wrong. He placed the tanks in the corner so that they could be later secured after the ship's cargo hold was empty.

Jack was popular amongst the crew because he always managed to bring an extra stash of fresh fruit and other consumable treats from home. This trip, he brought two cases of rum cakes, which was a favorite of the crew. Unlike other baked goods, which did not keep well, the rum cakes could be stored for years and still taste as fresh as the day they were made, and the alcohol made them particularly enjoyable.

As Rex turned to leave, he noticed fire damage to the port side wing of Jack's ship. It was charred. Evidently, something unusual had happened during Jack's trip. Rex walked over to the wing for a closer look. The metal was melted in a straight line and Rex's first guess as to what had transpired was that Jack might have had a problem while landing, but then he saw the circular hole in the tail of the ship that could have only been made by a laser. He took a step forward to examine it more closely, and his suspicion was confirmed. The ship's damage could only have been caused by an act of aggression.

Rex glanced back to the spot where Ed and Jack were standing, but they were no longer there. Rex pointed out the ship damage to Kong, a young crewmember standing nearby. The scruffy young man examined it and concurred with Rex's conclusion. The crew continued working to unload Jack's ship, and the whispers grew as they also became aware of the damage.

Rex returned to his room to gather his thoughts. He sat down at his desk and engaged Pops to see if he had any more information about Jack's ship.

"Pops, any news?"

Pops's disembodied face appeared and glided around the room. "About what?"

"Please, don't do that. It's disturbing."

A body appeared below Pops's head, and he sat down on the bed.

"Thank you," Rex said, and he turned to address Pops. "You're no help if you haven't heard the news."

"So tell me the news," Pops said.

"Captain Jack arrived."

"That's not news."

"No, but it looks like his ship was attacked."

"Attacked?"

"There was damage to the body; it looks like a laser did it."

"Why in tarnation?" Pops stood back up and paced back and forth across the room.

"Why wouldn't there be any word of this yet Pops?"

"It's bad, that's why."

"Clearly," Rex said, "but there must have been some reports made already."

"They are buying time."

"Maybe," Rex said.

"Why don't you ask Jack?"

"I will when I see him," Rex said.

"You can ask him now, he's standing outside the door."

Rex went to the door to greet Jack. "Thanks," he said as he opened the door.

Jack was standing at the doorway about to knock and holding a bottle of eighteen-year-old Laphroaig single-malt Scotch. "How did you know this was for you?"

"I didn't," Rex said as he grabbed the bottle and retreated back into the room. "I wasn't talking to you." He set the bottle on his desk.

"Who else is here?"

"I was talking to Pops," Rex said.

"Oh," said Jack. "Tell Pops I said hello."

"He can hear you."

Rex walked over the closet and began rummaging around; looking for the set of tumblers that he had previously swiped from the cafeteria for such occasions.

"Still can't get used to this holographic tech stuff," Jack said as he walked through Pops's image that was still pacing back and forth in the room. Jack sat down in Rex's chair. Rex continued searching for the tumblers.

"They're in the bottom drawer of your desk," said Pops as he made the drawer slide open, "and you're welcome."

"Thank you," said Rex. Pops disappeared.

"For what?" Jack asked. "I already gave you the Scotch."

"Talking to Pops again," said Rex as he got up to look in the desk drawer where he found the steel tumblers.

"You should enable the audio on Pops; I'd like to hear what he has to say."

"Sorry, it's a security thing."

"Right, makes sense."

Rex opened the bottle of Scotch and filled the two glasses to the rim. As usual, Jack was all smiles. Rex gave him a quick pat on the back and handed him a cup. "Sorry, no ice."

"No worries, I prefer my Scotch neat," Jack said. "Sorry you can't have any, Pops!"

"He's gone now."

"Maybe you should put an electronic bell on him or something so people know if he's in or out at least."

Rex laughed and took a seat on his bed. "I don't think he'd take well to that." He took a sip of his drink. He was eager to ask Jack about the damage to his ship. "Rough trip?"

Jack smirked, revealing several tiny wrinkles around his mouth. He swirled his glass before he took another drink, while Rex sat impatiently waiting for his answer. Jack raised his glass in a toast as he looked toward the picture of Avery sitting on Rex's desk. "To Captain Avery, my captain, rise up." Jack always made a toast to Avery when he visited. Rex appreciated the gesture.

Rex raised his glass in kind and took a drink. It seemed that Jack was avoiding his question, so he asked again. "So, how was your trip?"

"Well, you saw what happened, right?"

"Yeah, but what the hell caused that to happen?" Rex moved forward to better hear Jack's explanation.

"They shot at me. Damn Russians shot at me."

Jack stood up and recounted his tale demonstratively. "They had a blockade set up, just like they've been threatening to do. I played chicken with one of their flying junk heaps, and he locked his laser on me and fired! I flew right over the top of his ship and hoped for the best."

"Why would they shoot at you though?"

"I don't know, and I don't care."

"How's your ship?"

Jack sat back down. "She'll still fly."

"Are you still going back tomorrow?"

"Yes, I'm going back tomorrow."

"Shouldn't you stay, given the situation?"

"I need to get back before they launch more flying dinghies to get me."

"What are they saying on the ground?" Rex asked.

"So far they're acting like nothing happened."

"How's that possible?"

"You know," Jack said, "if a tree falls in the woods ..."

"But people will talk about it."

"Not for a while."

"Have you talked to Hendricks?"

Jack laughed. "Hendricks? You think he's going make a fuss? He wants me to get back as quickly as possible."

"What do they expect us to think up here?"

"Ed will take care of that," Jack said.

"What do you mean?"

"Ed will make a reassuring statement or something, and it will be business as usual up here, you'll see."

"But why would Ed do that?"

"You'll have to ask him," Jack said. "Ed's job is to keep the base running, nothing more."

Rex set down his drink. "But they shot at you."

"And they missed."

Rex looked at Jack incredulously. "They hit your ship."

"Barely," Jack said as he took a drink of his Scotch.

"What if they try it again?"

"We'll find out tomorrow."

"Where do you think this is all headed, Jack?"

"Hard to say. It all depends how far the Russians are willing to go. I don't know about these things, but I do know they are hell bent set on having an inspection."

"Ed said he wouldn't let them in."

"Well, it's going to be a fight then."

"For what?"

Jack swirled the liquid in his tumbler. "Control."

"Control of what?"

"The moon and its resources."

Rex shifted his sitting position as his right leg was tensing up. "Fighting over moon dust?"

"Among other things."

"Then why did they participate in building the base at all?"

"How could they not?"

"Right, but then why back out and cut funding to the base now and cause all these problems?"

"I suppose they hoped everyone would leave," Jack said.

"Wouldn't it be easier to cooperate as originally planned?"

Jack finished his Scotch. "People have fought over land and resources for eons, why would you expect it to stop on the moon?"

"I hope you're wrong, Jack." Rex wanted to talk to Ed straightaway. He stood up. "Let's walk over to the lounge. I need to go find Ed, and you can catch up with Mei while I go talk to him."

"Yes, it's not polite to keep a lady waiting." Jack set his cup down on the desk.

They walked out of the room and down the corridor to the lounge. Mei was already sitting at a table in the corner, waiting for Jack. Rex motioned to Jack that he was off to see Ed, and Jack nodded to acknowledge Rex's departure.

Rex took his time walking down the corridor as he reflected on the situation. He did not appreciate the lack of information about the attack on Jack's ship. They all deserved to know the truth about any risk to them or their safety.

He entered the control room and looked for Ed, but he was not there. A number or technicians were busy at their consoles. "Where's Ed?"

Wes, Ed's second in command, answered from across the room: "He's off duty." Rex turned around and went directly to Ed's room. He knocked twice and entered without waiting for a response. Upon entry, Rex realized his mistake. Ed immediately jumped up from his bed, and grabbed a sheet to cover himself. Judith sat up with the rest of the covers draped over her torso.

"What are you doing here?" Judith asked with horrified look on her face.

Rex was taken aback by the scene, but he did not leave. "I need to talk to Ed."

Ed approached Rex, motioning for him to get out. They stepped out of the room into the hall. "Not a good time, Rex."

"Aren't you going to talk to us about the attack on Jack's ship?"

"Didn't Jack tell you?"

"Unofficially, yes."

"We're not official here, Rex, you know that."

"Shouldn't you tell the rest of crew about the attack?"

Ed's face flushed and he started speaking in a low but stern voice. "Everyone knows already, what else can I add?"

"Anything would be better than silence."

"Look, nobody knows what's going on. We think communications have been jammed. We're working on it."

"And that's not important to tell us?"

"I don't answer to you, Rex."

"But you owe the crew some answers."

"There aren't any, so go get the shipment ready so that Jack can leave here early tomorrow."

"That's it?"

"For now." Ed stepped back inside of his room and abruptly shut the door. As Rex turned to leave, Ed came back out. "One more thing." Ed hastily raised his right fist and landed it firmly on Rex's left cheek, causing him to stumble back and hit the wall behind him. "Don't ever barge into my room again." Before Rex could react, Ed had retreated back to his room and shut the door.

Rex charged the door and struck it. "What the hell, Ed?" shouted Rex. He then took a few breaths before leaving the scene. He considered going after Ed but then thought the better of it. Rex realized as he stood in the hallway still in his slouched position that perhaps he could have picked a better time to confront Ed. He clenched his teeth and walked away to rejoin Jack in the lounge.

❖

Rex spent the rest of the evening with Jack and Mei playing Jack's favorite game, rummy. Jack did not know how to play mahjong and had no interest in learning. They always humored him. After the second game of rummy, Rex could see that Mei was cozying up to Jack. He left the table and joined Feng Feng, who had just sat down across the room. Feng Feng did not even acknowledge his presence when he sat down. Rex nudged him.

"Why didn't you come join us?" He could not wait to tell him about his scuffle with Ed.

"I needed to think," Feng Feng said.

"About what?"

"I heard that Jack's ship was attacked."

"Yes, it was," Rex said.

"So what does this mean?" Feng Feng threw up his hands. "Why doesn't Ed tell us something?"

Rex relayed his recent confrontation with Ed in the hallway.

"Why can't Ed just let the Russians come and inspect? If there's nothing going on here, why not?"

"I don't think it's ultimately Ed's decision," Rex said.

"The United States is being stubborn at our expense."

Rex did not want to disparage the U.S. government, but he tended to agree with Feng Feng's sentiments. He tried to change the subject. "There's one thing we can do to make it better."

"What's that?" Feng Feng asked.

Rex stood up and motioned for Feng Feng to follow him.

Feng Feng obliged. "Where are we going?"

"Just come with me."

They walked out of the lounge and passed by Jack and Mei, who were both too engrossed with one another to notice them leaving. Rex was happy that Mei was able to find someone of comfort to her after Quon. For a brief moment, he wondered if he would ever do the same. Rex walked briskly down the corridor before looking back. He turned his head around to see whether Feng Feng was behind him, and in fact he was. They both entered the hangar and the lights slowly flickered on.

"What are we doing here?"

"Look," Rex said, pointing to Jack's ship. Rex walked over to the port side of the ship and pointed out the charred metal to Feng Feng. "This wasn't a warning shot, they could have killed him."

Feng Feng placed both of his hands on the metal and slid them across the wing. "Is he going to fly back like this?"

"Yeah, he thinks it's fine," Rex said as he walked over to the storage locker.

"It could break clean off at any moment!"

"I know," Rex said.

"He's one lucky duck."

Rex grabbed two sets of welding goggles from the locker and threw a pair to Feng Feng. "He still has to make it back tomorrow." Rex took two plasma welders and walked back over the ship, handing one to Feng Feng.

"What am I supposed to do with this?"

"Watch." Rex began welding the already scorched metal, trying to smooth out the surface. Feng Feng did the same on the opposite side of the wing across from Rex.

"Do you think they'll try it again?" Feng Feng asked.

"Hope not."

"What if they do?"

"It could start a war," Rex said.

"What do you think they will do to us up here if that happened?"

"Since they want to inspect, I suppose they'll come a knocking, and Ed might try to resist."

Feng Feng shook his head and stopped talking. Rex and Feng Feng worked on the ship for two and a half hours. When they had tentatively finished, they agreed to meet back in the hangar for a second look at the wing, an hour before Jack's scheduled departure, to make sure that it was solidly secured.

Rex was exhausted when he retired to his room. He walked in and did not even notice Ed sitting in his chair, drinking some of the Scotch that Jack had left until he spoke. "Sorry about earlier," Ed said. "I overreacted."

Rex was startled. "What the hell, Ed? I only wanted some answers." He flopped down on his bed. "What's really going on here?"

"I don't know," Ed said.

"Come on, someone at the company must have told you *something*."

"They've said lots of things, and I still don't know anything, and now the communication systems are down."

"What did Hendricks say before the communications went down?"

Ed offered some Scotch to Rex, which he refused. "He said they want Jack to take the shipment back tomorrow."

"He can't go back."

"He's going," Ed said. "I talked to Jack."

"It's not safe."

"He'll be fine."

Rex was skeptical. "You really think that?"

"It would be foolish to fire at Jack's ship again," Ed said.

"What if they do?"

"Then we can start to worry." Ed stood up walked out.

Rex slipped off his shoes and curled up on his side as he reached for his pillow. He didn't even bother to get himself under the covers. He closed his eyes and was unconscious before he could reflect on the day's events.

CHAPTER NINE

BY THE TIME Rex got up and made his way to the hangar, Feng Feng was nearly finished working on the ship's wing. Rex secured the helium tanks and locked them in place for the journey back. Then he walked over to the port side to look over the wing again. Rex ran his hand over the surface of the wing and found the metal to be smooth, as it should be.

Feng Feng jumped down from the wing and removed his safety goggles. "It's as good as new."

"Nice work," Rex said. He was relieved to see that the wing was sturdy enough for the voyage back. He found it hard to comprehend how the Russians could turn to violence so quickly, but then it occurred to him that even he and Ed had come to blows quite suddenly. For Jack's sake, he hoped that level heads would prevail today.

Jack sauntered in to the hangar and walked over to them. He smiled and ran both of his hands over their work. "I knew you guys were up to something." Jack grabbed Feng Feng and hugged him and then he nabbed Rex.

"We couldn't let you leave like that," Rex said.

"I've flown worse," Jack said.

Rex closed the hatch on the cargo hold. "Not up here."

Feng Feng held out his hand to Jack and bid him a safe journey home. Then Feng Feng made a quick exit, as he was already late in checking on his solar panels. Rex continued to linger by the shuttle as Jack put on his flight suit. "Are you sure you want to go?"

"I've got to keep my schedule," Jack said.

"Shouldn't you wait until we hear something about the blockade?"

"No time to waste."

"But they could shoot at you again."

Jack was now fully suited and ready to go. "I know."

"There's no reason to put yourself at risk."

"You just loaded up ten billion reasons."

"Just wait until we hear something from the ground," Rex said.

"That could take days, even weeks."

"So?"

"Time is money."

"Come on, Jack."

"I'll see you next month."

"Maybe we shouldn't have fixed your wing," Rex said.

"I'd leave anyway."

"I know," Rex said.

Jack stepped inside the ship. "Get out of here, you're making me nervous."

Rex waved good-by.

❋

Judith was hunched over the computer console when Rex walked in. He anticipated that she was upset over his unannounced entry into Ed's room the night before. He sat down at the console and pulled up the analysis of their prior fusion test. Judith ignored him. He was about to apologize when she turned and looked him directly in the eyes. "You've been up here a long time; maybe you should start to think about going home."

Rex swallowed his apology and commenced verbal combat with her instead. "Maybe, but Ed doesn't have the guts to send me home." Judith's normally pale visage turned pink and the base of her neck became blotchy. He did not originally intend to goad her on, but she touched upon a particularly sore topic.

Judith turned to Rex. "Ed wanted to send you home today, but it was Jack's decision not to take passengers."

"Actually, just so you know, Ed came and apologized to me last night, and he had no problem with Hendricks sending you and me *both* home when he suggested it."

"I don't believe you," Judith said.

"Why don't you ask Ed?"

Rex did not want to argue with Judith. He found it unfortunate that they only seemed to get along outside of the fusion lab. Before Judith could respond, Feng Feng burst into the lab. He was wearing his environmental suit minus the boots and helmet, leaving his bare feet exposed. He was frantic.

Judith immediately confronted him. "You can't be in here! This is a restricted area."

Feng Feng ran to Rex. "Something's happened!"

Rex stood up to meet Feng Feng. "What's wrong?"

"There was an explosion."

"The generators?" Judith asked.

"No, in space, toward the White Tiger's legs," Feng Feng said.

Judith continued to question him. "What do you mean, White Tiger's legs? Are you all right?"

Rex explained while Feng Feng caught his breath. "He means in the direction of Andromeda. The Chinese constellations are the Black Tortoise to the North, Azure Dragon to the East, Vermillion Bird to the South, and White Tiger to the West. Andromeda galaxy is near the White Tiger's legs."

"There was a brilliant flash of red light, then orange, and then nothing."

"This was in Jack's flight path?" Rex asked.

"Yes, I was dusting off the solar panels when I noticed several flashes of light reflecting off the side of the panel. I turned to look behind me, and saw it."

"Jack's ship?" Judith asked.

Feng Feng did not answer. His eyes were wide and he bit his lower lip.

Judith went back to the console to check whether communications had been restored. She confirmed that they were not. "Maybe Ed has news." Rex and Feng Feng looked to Judith for further instruction. She closed the program she was working on and then quickly motioned for them to follow her as she walked toward the exit. Rex and Feng Feng walked behind her, allowing her to lead the way to the control room.

When they entered the control room, none of the personnel acknowledged their presence. The staff was fully occupied, trying various methods of contacting the Moon-X headquarters. Despite the frenzied level of activity, it was apparent that Ed was not in the room. Judith approached Wes. "Where's Ed?"

"He's resting and asked not to be disturbed."

Judith took his words as a challenge and walked out of the room with singular purpose.

Wes ran into the hall after her. "No, really, he's not to be disturbed!"

Judith brushed him aside and kept walking. Wes looked at Rex and Feng Feng as if to implore their assistance. Rex continued to follow Judith. Wherever she was going, he was following, and so was Feng Feng.

When they reached Ed's door, Judith went inside and Rex and Feng Feng waited in the hallway. As soon as she entered they heard a woman shriek. Rex was startled. He looked at Feng Feng. "Should we go in?"

Before they could move, Judith reappeared and ran down the hallway. Rex and Feng Feng looked at each other for direction. Ed appeared in the doorway and as he opened the door wider, they saw Helen, one of the technology specialists, inside. Ed had once again been caught in his over-zealous extracurricular activities. Ed stood shirtless in the doorway. Rex could not resist the opportunity to comment. "Bad time again, Ed?" Ed looked at Rex as if he wanted to deck him for the second time. Rex backed away. "We just wanted to know what happened to Jack."

"Jack?" Ed asked.

"Yes," Rex said. "Feng Feng saw an explosion."

Feng Feng chimed in, "It was a bright flash of light in the shuttle path."

Ed regained his composure. "Did you talk to Wes?"

"We were looking for you," Rex said.

"I haven't heard," Ed said. "I'll try to tap into Kaguya. Maybe the Japanese satellite can tell us something."

Feng Feng had a confused look on his face. "Japanese satellite? Didn't they abandon all of their lunar activities?"

"Yes," Ed said, "but they did not bother to decommission their probes and satellites, so Kaguya's lunar radar and plasma imager could still be functional."

Rex was hopeful about this new information, although it might only confirm his fears about Jack. Ed retreated back inside of his room. Rex and Feng Feng walked together down the corridor in the direction of the crew's quarters. Rex suggested they find Judith. Feng Feng agreed, and they went to her quarters. They knocked. Hearing no answer, they peeked inside. Judith was sitting on the edge of her bed with her head between her knees.

Judith looked up when they entered. "I had heard the stories about him," she said, "but I never thought he'd do this to me."

Feng Feng approached her. "Do not fret over him, this was not a love match."

Rex stepped farther inside Judith's pristine lair. "Are you okay, Judith?" He tried to be kind.

Judith looked away. "I just need a moment; I'll be fine."

Rex placed the palm of his hand on her back as he finally uttered the apology he tried to give her in the lab, only now it was in a different context. "I'm sorry."

"No, I'm sorry, Rex," Judith said. "Thank God you weren't on that shuttle, too. Go find Mei before she hears the news from someone else."

"She's right," Feng Feng said. "You go. I'll stay with Judith."

Rex found Mei in the cafeteria having an early lunch. He sat down next to her and asked her to take a walk with him. Reluctantly, she obliged and they walked over to the lounge, where Rex sat Mei down on the empty sofa in the back of the room. Rex did not know where to start. However, Mei, being very intuitive, spoke first. "Did something happen to Jack?"

"We don't know for sure," Rex said, "but Feng Feng saw something."

Mei's lips pursed and her eyes became glossy, as if on the verge of tears. "What?"

"He was outside checking the solar panels and he saw an explosion in the shuttle's flight path. There's still no communication with the ground to confirm anything."

"I had a bad feeling today. I asked him not to leave." Reluctant tears fell from Mei's eyes. Rex put his arm around her. Jack had been the only one able to reanimate Mei again after she had lost Quon on the *Minerva*. Rex wondered how Mei could possibly recover from such a compounded loss. He squeezed Mei tightly and buried his head on her shoulder as they both sat silently, just as they had done for many nights in Rex's room after the news of the *Minerva's* disappearance.

"I knew that Jack and I would not be together for long, but I did not expect him to die too," Mei said. "Maybe I'm cursed. I never dreamed a handsome western man would ever take an interest in a farm girl from Guizhou. If Quon was not also from there, I don't think even he would have married me. Now they're both gone."

Rex took Mei's hand. "Mei, you are no longer in Guizhou, and I don't think you've ever really been a farm girl."

Mei collapsed onto Rex's chest. "Talk to me, Rex. Say anything—tell me a story—anything to stop me from thinking about it."

"I don't know, Mei. I can barely think."

Mei sobbed in his arms. Rex held her and tried to think of something comforting to say. "Okay, let me tell you about the Goddess of the moon, Selene. One day, while Selene was riding her chariot across the sky, she saw a handsome young shepherd named Endymion, who was sleeping in a field. She was so taken by him that she stared at him all night—"

"Creepy," Mei said.

"Wait, it gets worse. Since he was a mortal, Selene knew that Zeus would not let her have him. So she went to Zeus and asked him to give Endymion eternal life and youth so she could gaze upon him forever."

"More creepy."

"Right, and Zeus granted her wish, but he made Endymion sleep for eternity in a suspended state. They say that as he slept, he dreamed that he held the moon in his arms forever."[4]

"Do you think they dream of us, Rex?"

"Yes," Rex said softly as he stroked Mei's long dark hair.

"How can you be sure?"

"Because I dream of her," Rex said.

"Who will Jack dream of?"

---

[4]   https://en.wikipedia.org/wiki/Endymion_(mythology); and see https://creativecommons.org/licenses/by-sa/3.0/ (adaptive changes made).

Rex tried to joke. "Many women."

Mei let out a faint laugh. "Yes, and many women will dream of him."

Rex liked the thought of Avery in a perpetual dream state as opposed to his vision of her in his nightmares involving her frozen corpse drifting aimlessly through dark space. Neither said another word until they heard the announcement from Ed that he had news to share with crew. He called for all hands to come to the cafeteria again for a briefing, which was becoming his way of delivering bad news.

"What do you think he's going to say?" Mei asked.

Rex was honest but gentle in his response. "Probably what we already know." Mei sat up and grasped at Rex's left arm.

They did not move to the cafeteria. Instead, they listened from the lounge. Rex had already seen enough of Ed for one day. Sensing that bad news was forthcoming, Rex wrapped his arm tighter around Mei. Ed addressed the crew. He explained what Feng Feng witnessed in the shuttle's flight path and that they could not make contact with the ground or with the space station to confirm the event. However, they confirmed through Kaguya, the Japanese probe, that the shuttle was not present on any of the images from its relay satellite. He stated the facts slowly and succinctly and urged everyone not to jump to conclusions, and said that he would keep the crew posted if there were any updates. Afterward, whispers replaced the usual loud conversations of the crew in the cafeteria.

"He's gone," Mei said.

Rex did not rebut her utterance. He was bothered by the fact that Ed offered no further guidance on how to proceed on the base or what precautions they might take. He remembered what Jack had said about it being Ed's job to keep the base running. However, Rex could not help but think that doing so might now be a futile endeavor.

CHAPTER TEN

R EX SAT IN the cafeteria sipping his lukewarm coffee and stirring a bowl of congee. He thought about the plans that he and Avery had to explore some of the craters on the moon before she left for her mission. They did not have enough time back then for such activities. Then it struck him that it might be a good idea to go out and explore now that communications were down and work was at a standstill. Rex disposed of his uneaten breakfast and went to find Feng Feng on the running track.

Feng Feng had a habit of going for a run every morning. Most of the crew preferred to use the exercise equipment in the small makeshift gym near the lounge, so the track was never crowded. In fact, the subterranean space was not designed for any use other than providing a foundation for the base. Nonetheless, the crew started using the oval-shaped room once it was discovered that they could install lighting. The outer dome covering the base was constructed around another inner dome, which insulated and protected the base. The foundation lay slightly outside of the inner dome. Subsequently, many people were hesitant to use the track because if the outer hull of the first dome were breached, this area would lose oxygen first. For this reason many people avoided this area. However, if something breached the outer hull, it would most likely get through the second hull, too. This area was also cooler than the rest of the base, which made it a slightly uncomfortable place to be for long periods of time, except while vigorously exercising.

Rex walked around the track in the direction of the thumping sound, which he assumed was coming from Feng Feng's feet. He approached the mural of Shanghai that Yelena and several of her friends had painted. It was Yelena's idea to cover the walls of the track with pictures of the representative cities of the collaborating governments, Shanghai, New York, and St. Petersburg. She told Rex that she intentionally did not choose any capital cities. In the gaps between the cityscapes Yelena painted Chinese, Russian, and English graffiti. This was Rex's favorite part of the mural. He especially liked the brightly colored Chinese characters randomly strewn about on the wall, ceiling, and air ducts. After she told him that these were actually profanities, he liked them even more. On one side of the wall there was a cityscape, and on the other, a walkway adjacent to each of the cities' iconic rivers: the Huangpu, Hudson, and Neva. The only area left unfinished was the ceiling. As Rex walked through the Bund area of the track, Feng Feng turned the corner.

Feng Feng slowed down and greeted Rex. "What brings you down here?"

"I wanted to propose a little outing."

Feng Feng approached Rex and turned around to walk with him in the opposite direction. "Where to?"

"Sverdrup," Rex said.

Feng Feng looked confused. "Sverdrup?"

"Yes," Rex said. "Sverdrup."

Feng Feng understood. "Brilliant! Yes, Sverdrup."

Rex and Feng Feng both smiled at each other as if they had made a great mutual discovery. "I almost did not get up this morning, I was feeling so down," Feng Feng said.

"I know, everything seems to be falling apart. First the *Minerva*, now Jack's shuttle, the blockade, no communications, what's next?"

Feng Feng did not respond.

Rex was excited about exploring the crater and gathering samples. No other craters, except for Shackleton Crater, had yet been explored. If they found more ice in Sverdrup Crater, it could allow future expansion on the moon to happen much more quickly.

"We can take the LRV," Rex said.

Feng Feng and Rex walked to the exit. "You go grab Pops to help us navigate out there," Feng Feng said, "and I'll clean up and meet you in the airlock." Rex agreed and they left going in their separate directions to prepare for their outing.

❀

Rex met Feng Feng in the changing room near the airlock. He took two helmets with attachment capabilities and rigged them so that they could carry imagers, which consisted of a monolaser, camera, and prism. The prism was able to bend the laser beam ninety degrees and then rotate it to broadcast a straight line across the terrain, allowing Pops to translate it into a three dimensional image. Until they reached the pitch-black interior of the crater, however, they could not use the imagers and would have to rely solely on the flashlights. It would also be extremely cold, so Rex and Feng Feng put on their extra-padded environmental suits that offered more thermal protection. They were bulkier than their regular suits, but Rex did not anticipate needing much agility for this excursion. They would only be mapping the floor of the crater and gathering rock samples. Because of the extra padding, these suits required them to strip down to their underwear. All of the environmental suits were also equipped with nanotechnology that monitored their internal functions and were able to make repairs or adjustments to their suits as needed.

Once fully suited, Rex and Feng Feng synced their helmets and tested them to make sure they were on the same frequency and could hear each other.

"You ready?" Rex asked.

"Can't wait."

Rex was eager to go exploring, but he also knew that with external communications being down they would be completely on their own, and nobody would be able to help them if they ran into trouble. He took extra supplies in case they might need anything. "Okay, then. We're off." They gave each other a nod, indicating that they were ready and then made their way through the airlock. Looking at the expansive lunarscape around him made Rex realize how static the base was starting to feel.

Rex and Feng Feng wanted to preserve as much of their oxygen as possible so as to have a longer walk in the crater; therefore they did not speak until they reached the crater. Normally Rex used the LRV to gather distant broken-down harvesters and was practically the only one who ever drove it. Today Rex allowed Feng Feng the pleasure of driving on the moon. The vehicle was not equipped with two seats, so Rex stood on the back and held on to the roll bar.

Riding the LRV on the moon was what he imagined riding a dune buggy through a desert at night on Earth would be like, and it was quite enjoyable. With no roads or paths, one could drive everywhere and arrive nowhere. The only constraint to free movement was the rocky terrain itself. Rex tried to imagine that they were riding in a convertible. The lack of atmosphere and the bulkiness of his suit, however, made this only a fleeting thought.

As they approached the crater, Feng Feng slowed down and rolled to a stop at the crater's rim. Unlike Shackleton Crater, which was almost perfectly round in shape, Sverdrup was kidney shaped—the product of multiple impacts. It was also five times as large as Shackleton. Feng Feng walked quickly over to the edge of the rim. There was still enough sunlight to see a ledge to which they could descend partway down into the belly of the crater, but from there they would have to blindly repel the rest of the way down into the abyss.

Rex turned on his helmet light and affixed his laser flashlight to his left arm before attaching Feng Feng's. Next, he attached one of the monolasers to Feng Feng's helmet and Feng Feng attached the other to Rex's. They would have to wait to turn on their laser flashlights since they needed their arms to repel down the ledge, and there was the added risk of burning each other with the heat of the high-powered beams. Therefore, they would have no way of knowing when they would reach the floor until they hit it.

Rex looked down the ledge. "Pops, can you get a reading on the depth?"

"Are you sure you want to go down there?" Pops asked. "It's so dark."

"Please, just tell me how far we need to go."

"Maybe about twelve hundred meters," Pops said.

"Maybe?"

"The bottom is uneven," Pops said, "so it's hard to get a clear reading."

Rex turned to Feng Feng. "Looks like quite a ways down. You ready?" Feng Feng nodded as he fastened their ropes to the base of the ledge. He jumped down before Rex could even ask who wanted to go first. Rex followed. They were both silent as they concentrated on making their way methodically to the bottom. With each jump, Rex could feel it grow colder for a few seconds before his environmental suit was able to adjust the temperature.

Feng Feng hit the ground first and warned Rex. Then Rex reached the bottom and fell backward. He stood up and stepped away from his rope. He looked for Feng Feng in the dark. He could only see him in the single beam of light from his helmet, which made him realize how enveloped by the darkness they were. Rex put reflectors on their dangling ropes while Feng Feng dropped some reflectors in the immediate area so they could find their way back more easily.

Rex handed Feng Feng a bag to collect some samples. "We only have thirty minutes; let's stay near the ledge. I'll go to the right and you go to the left."

"See you in thirty," Feng Feng said.

Rex proceeded forward, hugging the side of the crater wall. He adjusted his laser flashlight so that he need not hold his arm upright for the whole walk. Pops was able to supplement Rex's and Feng Feng's view of the terrain with readings from ground scans. The crater floor looked similar to the lunar surface above, but it was more rugged, and there were taller and more jagged rock formations resembling stalagmites. Rex stopped to pick up a rock sample every several steps. As he made his way, Rex began to feel very conscious of not being able to see what was on his left. Every time he tried to peer out in that direction, his light would only penetrate ten meters. Pops was unable to supplement the view in that direction because he could not find a reference point in the darkness.

"Any idea how wide the crater is?" Rex asked.

"Nope," Pops said. "You'd have to walk all the way around to figure that out."

"We don't have enough time for that."

"Then I guess you'll never know," Pops said.

Rex came upon a tall rock formation that he had to maneuver around. "Any idea what could have formed that?"

"Nope," Pops said.

"You're so helpful today, Pops. Maybe we should have left you on the base."

"Then you wouldn't have gotten Sergei's message," Pops said.

Rex stopped walking. "What message?"

"I received a message from the space station from Sergei while on our way to the crater."

"Why didn't you say anything?"

"I did not want to slow you down."

"But now it's okay?"

"Now I'm making myself useful, as you say," Pops said.

"What's the message?"

"Sergei says things are happening on the space station and that a large armed ship is on its way to the base. He says to be careful."

"Anything else?"

"Nope," Pops said.

"An armed ship?"

"That's what he said."

Rex continued walking. "How did you get the message? I thought we were blocked."

"Whatever is cutting off communications is not stopping communication outside of the base."

"Can we respond?"

"Probably not a good idea; your message might be intercepted."

"How did Sergei get around that?"

"Very carefully," Pops said.

"Okay, we'll have to discuss this later."

Rex tried to put Sergei's message out of his mind while he explored the crater, but it was nearly impossible not to wonder about the purpose of this armed ship. He wished that he could talk to Sergei in person. Rex continued to pick up some samples. As he bent down to gather a rock, Rex noticed a flicker of light coming from his left. He again pointed his laser light in that direction, which revealed a collection of reflective rocks. Intrigued, Rex veered away from the wall, deeper into the crater toward the alluring rocks.

"Don't take us out too far now," Pops said. "I don't want to get stuck out here."

"Me neither."

Rex reached the rocks and tried to get a better look at them. They did not seem to match the other darker colored rocks in the area. He gathered several of them and put them in his sack. He turned but did not return the same way from which he had come. Instead, he walked a little farther parallel to where he had found the rocks and then turned back toward the crater's perimeter. As he approached, he spotted what appeared to be a rectangular shape of a door in the wall of the crater. He moved closer for a better look. It became clear that there was a steel door built into the wall of the crater. A wave of disappointment flooded his stomach. They were not the first ones in the crater. Rex walked closer. A wide rock formation about waist high was in his way, and as he stepped around it, he felt his right foot become unsteady. He tried to regain his balance but found himself hurling forward. As he slowly descended to the ground, he wondered if every decision made on the moon was meant to result in misfortune. The next thing Rex knew, he was on the ground, and he felt the sting of the extreme cold in his left knee and then something moist and warm on his skin, then nothing.

CHAPTER ELEVEN

WHEN REX OPENED his eyes, Lucas, the medical assistant, was using surgical scissors to cut into the suit around his left knee. The top half of Rex's environmental suit had been removed, and his pale white torso was fully exposed while the bottom half of his suit was still on, minus his boots. Lucas was the only trained medic on the base. His job was to work as the hands of the medical residents who would watch and advise virtually from New York-Presbyterian Hospital in New York City. Since communications were blocked, Lucas was on his own. With all the careful planning that went in to designing and staffing the base, nobody foresaw that a simple communications failure could pose a threat to the safety of the crew.

Lucas stopped working when he saw Rex wake up. "Good, you're up. Now ya can help me make some decisions." Lucas was from Boston, and he spoke quickly and sounded as if all of his vowels flowed out of his nose instead of his lips. He had a full head of dark curly hair, and—although Lucas was thirty-eight—his chubby cheeks gave him a youthful, cherubic appearance.

Rex sat up. "Where am I?"

Lucas stepped back from Rex's leg. "You remember gettin' hurt?"

Rex nodded.

"Good, then your friend can explain how you got here. But to make it short, you jabbed your knee on some rocks and ripped your suit."

Rex motioned for him to keep explaining.

"The nanobots sealed the air leak, but there wasn't enough fabric to work with so the li'l buggas used your skin instead. Now, I can cut off the fabric around the stitching and cast up your leg until we can get to a doctor; or I can do the stitches myself, but I might cut some important parts in the process."

Rex stopped nodding. "What if you cut the fabric out now?"

Lucas stepped back over to Rex's knee. "If I cut out the fabric now, you'll walk outta' here with a limp, but I can't guarantee that there won't be permanent damage."

"Can the computer help you with the surgery?"

"It can guide the incisions, but I have no option other than to cut out the stitches, and this is no ordinary fabric."

"Let's do it," said Rex.

Lucas gathered his surgery kit. "What were you guys thinkin' going out to that crater?"

"I thought we were going to make some discoveries."

Lucas placed an oxygen mask over Rex's mouth. "What if the only discovery to be made is that we're not meant to be up here?" Rex disagreed, but he could not argue.

When Rex regained consciousness, Lucas was cleaning up his instruments. Rex's environmental suit was entirely off and he was wearing nothing but his briefs. He was cold and felt an intense stinging pain in his knee. "Hey, did you forget something in my leg?"

Lucas turned around to face Rex. "No, everything's accounted for. I'll give ya a shot for the pain." Lucas went back to placing his surgical tools in the sterilization case. He walked over to the medicine cabinet and drew up a syringe. Then, Lucas quickly walked back over to Rex and examined his knee, looking for a suitable spot to administer the injection. Rex watched with apprehension. Lucas plunged the needle into a red swollen lump above Rex's patella.

"How'd the surgery go?" Rex asked holding back a scream.

Lucas removed the syringe and placed it in a biohazard container. "Those 'bots really went to work on you. I had to cut through a lotta' tissue and some of your skin was frostbitten too, so I had to cut it off and then sew you up, and there wasn't much skin there to begin with."

Rex furrowed his brow. "Frostbite? Really? Didn't the nanobots fix me up within seconds?"

"Yes, but they still left some skin exposed. Without any protection, your bare skin froze up."

Rex squirmed on the table. "How much did you cut?"

"Don't worry, not enough to notice. I only had to scrape a few edges. Technically, you only had frostnip." Rex looked up at Lucas quizzically. Lucas continued, "That's the initial stage of frostbite—no cellula' degeneration. That Feng Feng was smart to wrap up your leg with a Mylar blanket. You should be able to hobble around."

"How long do I have to stay here?"

"You can get up anytime you feel like it." Rex was relieved to know that he would still be mobile. Lucas offered to call someone to help him to his quarters, but Rex refused. Lucas finished his cleanup of the area and set out a metal crutch for Rex to use. "Here, you're going to need this when you get up. I'm goin' to grab a drink. I'm not used to this surgery stuff." Lucas quickly left the room.

Alone on the table, Rex had time to reflect on his injury. He did not second-guess himself about going down into the crater, but he did question whatever bad decision he had made that landed him in the medical lab. Perhaps he should have stayed on the path along the rim of the crater. Then he thought about the door he saw and questioned whether it was real or imagined. He knew better than to ask Ed about it directly. He would have to sit on the information for a while, but he would have to tell Ed about the ship that Sergei warned him about. He guessed that Ed already knew about it. Rex waited to get up until the anesthetic took effect.

As Rex thought about the idea of frostnip in his knee, he was reminded of his college days—specifically when he was paired up with Avery for a thermodynamics lab experiment to calculate absolute zero. Avery's main focus was aeronautics and astronautics. Rex majored in nuclear physics and minored in geology. She was only taking the lab to fulfill her chemistry requirement. He only took the class because he enjoyed lab work as opposed to lectures.

At absolute zero, all molecular function was supposed to cease. The professor explained in an earlier class that scientists had never been able to reach absolute zero because the substance being measured always continued to have some level of molecular activity. The closest that scientists had been able to measure was -273 degrees Celsius. Scientists presumed this to be close to reaching absolute zero because they were able to show that the substance being measured exhibited superfluidity at this temperature, an indication that it was close to absolute zero. Rex wondered how cold his knee had gotten.

The experiment that Rex and Avery conducted consisted of taking a metal bulb and attaching it to a pressure gauge. Avery recorded the room temperature with an ordinary thermometer. She graphed the pressure in the bulb and the temperature of the room. Then they took the bulb and placed it in ice water and recorded the pressure in the bulb and temperature of the water. Avery marked the results on the graph. They repeated the process with boiling water, then alcohol, using a different thermometer that could not be damaged, and finally liquid nitrogen, but without using a thermometer. They were to assume the temperature to be -196 degrees Celsius and plot it on the graph accordingly. As expected the graph showed the pressure dropped with the temperature. They connected the points on the graph to extrapolate where absolute zero would fall. Their end point was -273 degrees Celsius. Upon completion of the experiment they concluded that the exercise was pointless since they already understood what the principle was that they were supposed to be discovering. After that lab, his study of thermodynamics was transformed into a study of all things Avery. Rex's mind was drawn back to this time for some reason. The knowledge that absolute zero reduced molecular movement is what made Rex aware of the fact that cold fusion was a farce, so he never pursued that line of experimentation.

Rex turned his attention back to the pain in his knee. The shot wasn't working yet, but he was eager to get going. He sat up, slid his leg over the side of the table, and hopped over to the other side of the room to put on the uniform that Lucas left for him. Once dressed, he grabbed the crutch and made his way out to the corridor. Shooting pains ran up his thigh with each deliberate step. Rex lifted up his left leg to keep his weight off of it, but holding his leg up in a bent position only increased his discomfort. He continued to make his way down the corridor. Although Rex wanted to find Feng Feng to thank him for bringing him back, he needed to return to his quarters to lie down and rest his leg. He also wanted to talk to Pops privately about Sergei's message and the door in the crater before going to Ed.

Rex took his time and tried to move his leg in all different directions in an attempt to find the least painful position. Keeping the leg straight and slightly in front of the right leg was the most comfortable position, and Rex could maneuver himself with the crutch the fastest this way. He reached his quarters and sat on the chair by the desk, leaving the crutch on the floor. He removed the nanodot from behind his ear to plug Pops back into his computer. He called out to Pops. "What happened?"

Pops's big green face appeared, hovering next to Rex. "I saved you, that's what happened."

"You?" Rex laughed. "I'm sure that Feng Feng dragged me back to the base."

"Who do you think told Feng Feng what to do?"

"Okay …right …thanks, Pops. Did you see that door in the crater?"

"Yes. I scanned it."

A slight chill came over Rex as Pops confirmed that the door really existed. "What do you make of it?"

"B-2 steel," Pops said.

"Super-steel? What do you think that means?"

"It's a strong door."

"Seriously, Pops, someone must be hiding something pretty important down there."

"I would forget that you saw anything if I were you."

"I can't."

"Me neither," Pops said.

"What should I do?"

"Nothing."

"I guess I'll have to sleep on it," Rex said.

"You're welcome," Pops said.

"Thank you, Pops."

Pops disappeared.

Rex scooted himself over to his bed. He continued to think about the door. Only the U.S. government would have had the time and capability to install a super-steel door in that crater, and they must certainly be hiding something important behind it. Rex puzzled over it until he dozed off.

❧

Mei and Feng Feng stopped by Rex's room, interrupting his nap. Rex was relieved to see Feng Feng, since it meant that he would not have to make the trek to his quarters to talk to him. He wanted to ask Feng Feng whether he saw the door in the crater, but since Mei was with him, he decided to wait. If Feng Feng did see something, Rex figured it was best to keep Mei out of it. He sat up from his slouched position. Mei came over first to hug him.

Feng Feng patted Rex on the back. "Glad to see you're up again."

"Thank you for dragging me back to the base," Rex said.

"Of course," Feng Feng said. "How's your leg?"

Rex stretched out his leg and pushed up his pant leg for them to see. Mei sat down on the bed next to Rex, while Feng Feng grabbed the chair from the corner and slid it closer to them. Mei examined Rex's knee, which was red and swollen. She touched the skin just below his femur and Rex flinched. "Sorry."

"It's okay," Rex said. "I'm starting to get used to the stabbing pain." He turned his attention to Feng Feng. "How did you get me back up the crater?"

Feng Feng sat back in his chair and recounted how Pops contacted him and guided him to Rex's location. Feng Feng reached into his pocket and presented Rex with one of the rocks he was chasing when he fell. "The rest are in the mining lab for you to play with later."

Rex could not stop smiling as he held up the rock to the light. "Interesting! Neither basalt nor anorthocite. It's got the classic olivine crystals surrounded by an iron-nickel matrix. I believe it's a part of a pallasite meteor."

Mei took a closer look. "It's very beautiful, whatever it is."

Feng Feng leaned forward to examine the rock. "Well, you can have fun classifying all your new rocks."

Rex grinned. "I will. This is a rare find."

"Okay," Feng Feng said jokingly, "how rare is it?"

Rex handed the sample to Mei. "If it's what I think it is, there have been less than seventy found on Earth to date."

Mei examined the specimen, shifting the rock from hand to hand. "Do you know how old it is?" She handed it back to Rex.

Rex held the rock up in the air. "About four and a half billion years old. Possibly a relic from the time of the forming planets."

"Why is it so rare?" she asked.

"Normally, a meteor doesn't survive its descent through the earth's atmosphere, but here on the moon, you don't have such a problem."

"So there might be more of them here?" Mei asked.

"Yes."

After passing the meteorite around a few more times, Mei and Feng Feng took their leave from Rex so he could rest. Unfortunately, by the time they left, the pain in Rex's knee was the worst it had been since he had woken up. Rex did not have the energy to go back to the medical bay. He called out for Pops to contact Lucas for another shot. Lucas came by, about twenty minutes later, with a syringe full of anesthetic. The needle shook in Lucas's hand as he plunged it into Rex's swollen knee. Rex was grateful for Lucas's attention, even though it was obvious that Lucas was inebriated.

CHAPTER TWELVE

BEFORE GOING TO the mining lab, Rex made his way down the corridor to see Ed. He loathed going to see him, given what had transpired every other time he knocked on his door, but he needed to talk to him about Sergei's message and the communications issue. His knee was still inflamed, and every step forward stirred up new pain, and leaning on the crutch only gave him minimal relief.

Rex focused his attention on reaching his destination instead of his discomfort. As he rounded the final corner, he kept the door of Ed's quarters as his target with each step he took. When he was halfway to his destination, the door opened, and Judith appeared. Rex was confused for a moment because he did not expect to see her with Ed after what had happened. Judith seemed to be equally taken aback by Rex's presence in the hall. He immediately understood the awkwardness of the situation. The last time he saw Judith, she was reeling from learning firsthand about Ed's womanizing ways.

Rex was incredulous that Ed could have said or done anything to regain her full trust and confidence. Their eyes locked, and there was nowhere for Rex to go to avoid Judith's passage, nor for her to avoid his. "Everything okay, Judith?" Without answering, she turned her head downward and walked briskly past him. Rex shook his head in disbelief.

Rex reached Ed's door and knocked. Ed opened the door, welcomed Rex inside, and asked him to take a seat. Rex did so, slowly placing his crutch on the floor next to his chair. He surmised that Ed must have been spending a lot of time in his quarters lately, given the number of empty and half-empty coffee cups on the desk. Before Rex could tell Ed about the communication capability outside of the base, Ed admonished him for his trip to the Sverdrup Crater.

"You know, you're lucky you made it back," Ed said, looking at Rex's leg. "You were supposed to let someone at the base know you were going out."

Rex was fully aware of the safety policy, but since communications were out already, there did not seem to be a point of giving notice of the outing. Nonetheless, Rex tried to placate Ed. "Yes. I should have let someone know."

Ed sat down and picked up one of the cups from his desk and drank. There were so many cups on the desk that Rex was not sure how Ed knew which one was fresh. "You should have that leg looked at by some real doctors. You might want to think about going home once things calm down here."

"We'll see. When do you suppose the next shuttle is coming, and who is going to want to pilot it after what happened?"

"Could be a while," Ed said. "There's no way to know what's going on down there now."

"I think I found a way."

"How?"

"While I was outside with Feng Feng, I received a message from Sergei on the space station. Whatever is blocking the communications is only targeting the base and satellites. If we set up transmitters outside, they might be able to send and receive messages."

Ed set down his cup. "Looks like we've finally got work to do." He stood up as if he was ready to go to work on the communication system right away.

"Wait. In Sergei's message, he said there's an armed ship on its way here. Do you know anything about this?"

Ed shook his head and made no further inquiry from Rex, which made Rex suspicious. "You think they're going to attack?"

"No, just more threats," Ed said.

"So far the Russians have made good on those threats."

"True."

Rex was bothered that Ed did not seem overly concerned. "Shouldn't we ask for help?"

"I'll let Hendricks know when I get through. We'll see what he says."

Ed helped Rex up out of his chair. They left Ed's quarters together and then parted. As Rex slowly made his way down to the mining lab, he wondered if Ed knew something that he was not sharing.

※

Rex examined the rock and meteor samples that Feng Feng had brought back. He was pleased that there were so many good samples of the pallasite meteorite. It was a noteworthy lunar find, and he felt it somehow made their excursion worthwhile despite his injury. Rex had barely finished logging and classifying all of the new samples when the communications systems began functioning again. He knew that the systems were restored because the computer in the lab started beeping and making the sounds it made it when it was receiving data. He put the rock samples away.

Since communications had been restored, Rex wanted to get to the fusion lab as quickly as possible. He was not eager to see Judith. He was embarrassed for her and concerned about her self-destructive behavior. He could not imagine Ed making apologies or pleading for her forgiveness, but it was equally as difficult to envisage Judith running back to Ed without some conciliatory gesture on his part. Either way, he understood it was not his place to judge.

※

Judith was standing up and talking to Ty in his holographic form when Rex entered the lab. They both turned their attention toward him as he slowly approached. Ty inquired about Rex's injury. Rex, however, was too eager for news from Earth to fill in Ty on the trip to the Sverdrup Crater. "I'm fine—I'll fill you in later. We're dying for news up here; tell us what's going on."

Ty stepped toward Rex. "I was just telling Judith that things aren't going so well down here at Moon-X."

"Why?" Rex asked. "What's going on?"

"They want you to suspend the fusion program for now. The Russians are saying that you are weaponizing the moon and unless you allow them in to inspect the lab, they are going take retaliatory action."

"They should know that we aren't doing anything with weapons in the fusion lab," Judith said.

Ty turned and moved toward Judith. "That's why the U.S. military says it's a ruse to disrupt our operations."

"What are the Chinese saying?" Judith asked.

"They want you to let the Russians in," Ty said.

"Why can't we do that?" Rex asked.

"Because the military says the Russians only want to spy."

"That doesn't make sense," Rex said.

Ty threw his hands in the air, swinging one of them through Judith's left shoulder. "But that's what they're saying."

"And now we're going to stop our work just like they want?" Rex asked.

"No," Ty said. "We will continue working down here at the Nevada facility."

"What does Hendricks want us to do up here, then?" Judith asked.

"Wait," Ty said.

"That's all we've been doing," Judith said.

Rex thought about the door in the crater. "Ty, what if the Russians are correct? What if the military is weaponizing the moon?"

Ty paused. Rex keenly observed the expression on Ty's face and noticed that he swallowed hard, almost a gulp. "That would change every-thing, wouldn't it?"

"Yes, and then everything would make sense, wouldn't it?"

Ty turned away. "I don't see how there could be weapons on the moon."

"The military was here first," Rex said, "before Moon-X and its crew."

Ty turned back around. "There's no point worrying about it. We all work for Moon-X, and we have to trust them and the military right now."

Rex changed the subject. "Have you heard anything about a large Russian ship headed our way?"

"Yes," Ty said. "It was launched about the same time the coms went down. It docked at the space station. We don't know much more about it."

Judith's eyes widened and she inhaled loudly. "Shouldn't the military get up here?"

"They don't want to risk another incident with the blockade," Ty said.

Judith shook her head. "Unbelievable. Send the Starfighters up here for nothing, but ground them when the base is under threat."

Rex thought Ty might know more than he was saying, so he pressed on. "What else did you hear?"

"Just rumors," Ty said.

"Such as?"

"I heard that the Russians want to test a new space weapon."

"Let me get this straight," Judith said. "They accuse us of making weapons in our lab, but they put a new space weapon into orbit?"

"There is no treaty addressing the use of defensive weapons in space, only the moon." Ty said.

"Who's attacking?" Judith asked. "That's the question."

Rex agreed with Judith. "Exactly, and what defensive weapon can't be used offensively?"

"What are we going to do?" Judith asked.

"The company wants to ramp up the work down here," Ty said.

"So they don't care about us up here anymore, then?" Rex asked.

"They care about the helium-3, don't forget," Ty said.

"Yeah, but they can afford to let us stew up here while you work out the details down there," Rex said.

"This will blow over," Ty said. "I'm sure of it."

Rex had nothing else to say. They were in lunar limbo until the governments came to some resolution about the operation of the base. Rex and Judith finished their conversation, Ty disappeared, and the room became silent.

Rex sat down and tried to engage Judith. "I still want to run another test."

Judith sat down next to Rex. "That's irresponsible."

"Look who's talking about being irresponsible."

"At least I know what I'm doing up here. Do you?" Judith snapped back.

"I'm here to find answers," Rex said. "What about you?"

Judith shook her head. "You don't get it, do you?"

"Get what?"

"I can't leave him."

Rex softened his demeanor. "Judith, he's not good for you; and you're too smart for that type of nonsense."

"Since when have brains ever been a defense to charm?"

"You can't be serious."

"He's all I have."

"That can't be true."

"I don't need your condescending advice. I've gone over and over this, and let's just assume it is true."

"Then you can do better."

"Nobody's perfect, Rex."

"I'm not here to argue with you, it's just hard to watch."

"Have you looked in a mirror lately?" Judith asked.

"I know I've let myself go, but I can fix that with a quick shave. It's only superficial."

"Are you sure?"

Rex did not want to continue the conversation with Judith. Perhaps she fully understood that she was walking into a foolhardy situation and had done so deliberately, but it was still distressing to observe a wounded animal fall prey to a predator. Instead of antagonizing her further, Rex remained quiet. He decided it was not the right time to ask Judith to run another test in defiance of Hendrick's orders. He would revisit the issue another time.

CHAPTER THIRTEEN

REX DISAGREED WITH the company's decision to stop work in the fusion lab. He considered running a test on his own, but this would be difficult without Judith's expertise. In order to be productive, Rex went to the Russian lab. He pulled up the control pad and removed Pops's nanodot from behind his ear and placed it into the gel. He rubbed his hands together to get rid of the excess goo.

Pops appeared, wearing a navy blue Russian uniform. "Back again?"

"Yes, Pops, but why are you wearing that?"

"I want to look official."

"Nobody can see you."

"That's your fault."

"It's not my *fault* Pops, it's how you were made."

"Like I said—"

Rex cut him off to curtail the argument. "Let's review the ship's coordinates and flight path."

"They were on their way to Mars."

Rex did not even bother to address Pops's sarcasm. "Can you look into where the ship would have been if they had not made the course correction?"

"You want me to guess where they might have been if they did not alter their course?"

"Yes."

"Why?

"Let's just see," Rex said.

"All I can give you is an approximation, since we do not know at what point the ship failed and how far it actually got. We also cannot account for other changes made after we lost contact, if there were any."

"Agreed. Let's check anyway."

"You know, you are clogging my memory with this data." Pops sat on top of the console.

"I'll get you more," Rex said.

Pops folded his arms. "What if I don't want more of this data?"

"That's not for you to choose."

"Oh? In that case it might be time for me to run a systems diagnostics check."

"You're fine, Pops."

"I don't know, all this Russian data is foreign to me."

"What do you want now, Pops?"

"Something new to think about. I'm bored with this." Pops lay down on top of the console.

"Pops, please, not now. We'll be leaving the base soon, and I can do more for you at home. Until then, we need to stay focused."

Pops sat up and hopped off of the table. "I am focused, are you?"

"Of course I am."

Pops stepped in front of Rex. "Really? Then why are we here?"

Rex put his hands in front of him as if to push Pops away but instead they went through the image of Pops's chest. "You're too close. Remember what I said about personal space?"

Pops whisked himself to the back of the room. "Is this far enough for you?"

"Get back here. Stop playing around."

Pops moved halfway back. "I'm just doing what you asked."

"No, you're not," Rex said, "and you know they suspended the fusion work."

"And the mining lab, why can't we mine?"

"No need to mine more right now."

"Why don't you finish analyzing your lunar samples, then?"

"I will," Rex said.

"When?"

"I don't answer to you, Pops."

"To whom do you answer, then?"

"Hendricks."

"And what does Hendricks want you to do?"

"Wait."

"Then let's wait," Pops said.

Rex rolled his eyes. "Just chart the course."

"No," Pops said.

"What?"

"You heard me."

"Pops, chart the course."

"What's the point?"

"To find out what happened."

"Why?"

"To know," Rex said.

"But you'll never know," Pops said.

"Only if you keep refusing to help."

"It's impossible to know anything without the physical debris."

"Maybe not."

"It's impossible."

"I don't care," Rex said.

"But what's the point?"

"To know what happened."

"But we can't know," Pops said.

"Maybe we can."

"Maybe it's something you will never know," Pops said.

"But I want to know, and I'm not going to stop looking. You wouldn't understand, Pops."

"What is that supposed to mean?"

"Never mind."

Rex took a deep breath and considered for a moment how to deal with Pops's obstinacy. The only successful way he'd found in the past was bribery. The result of this, however, only produced more demands and more frequent requests. Rex knew he needed to impose some discipline, but Pops never responded well to such. When he had previously attempted to do so, by keeping Pops contained in his personal system, Pops threw what could only be described as a tantrum and scrambled all of Rex's office files. Rex was beholden to his spoiled creation.

"We'll go to the mining lab later," Rex said. "You can help analyze the samples."

"That's nothing new."

"Okay. I'll plug you into the main system, and you can catch up on the news."

Finally Pops agreed, and they began charting the *Minerva's* uncorrected flight path. Pops produced a holographic image of the *Minerva's* actual flight path and Rex watched as Pops added lines to show where they had diverged. Rex figured this had to do with the space turbulence he had previously discovered. Maybe he had to accept that they would never know anything new about its disappearance, but if he were to quit, the *Minerva* would truly be lost.

Rex remembered the day the *Minerva* had left. Avery refused to admit how nervous she was. She never verbalized any misgivings or hesitations about the mission, but Rex had recognized her nervous symptoms—her inability to sleep despite turning in early, taking longer showers, and lack of focus on conversation whenever he tried to steer the topic to any subject other than Mars. She behaved the same way the week before her interview with the board for the captain's position. He learned more that week about Mars and its two moons, Phobos and Deimos, than he had in his entire life. Avery explained to him how the moons of Mars were more likely to be captured asteroids and how she looked forward to studying them up close. Rex did not mind learning about the Martian moons; he already knew so much about the earth's moon that any talk about other moons was refreshing. It was Avery's way of managing her nerves and Rex had played along.

Rex went through the ship's log once more. He convinced Pops to pull up the data for him, and together they went through the entries from the final month of the *Minerva's* mission. Once finished, Rex took Pops to the mining lab, where he plugged him in to the main database so Pops could catch up on the latest news.

❈

Rex's knee was starting to hurt again, and most of the crew had already turned in for the night. He needed to rest his leg. He headed toward his quarters but then turned to go to Mei's. Rex rarely visited her quarters, but tonight he did not feel like being alone. When he reached Mei's doorway, she was already at the door waiting for him. She must have heard him struggling with his crutch making his way down the hall. She welcomed him inside. The room was dark.

"I thought that was you," Mei said. Rex rested his crutch against the wall. Mei went to her closet and brought out an extra pillow. "Are you okay?"

"Yes, thanks. Do you mind having some company tonight?"

Mei got back into bed and opened the covers for Rex. She turned around as he undressed. After Rex tucked himself in, Mei sat up and placed a pillow under the covers behind Rex's knee to prop it up for him.

"How are you holding up?" Rex asked.

"Better, I think," Mei said. "It helps that communications are working again."

"Any other news from your contacts in Beijing?"

"My contact said that the U.S. military is in charge of Moon-X now. Do you think it's true?"

"Yes."

She held him a little tighter. "Are you ready to go home?"

"No, are you?"

"I need to finish my work up here. I can't imagine what will happen to me if I don't, especially now without Quon."

"You never planned a future with Jack?"

"No, that never seemed like a possibility."

"It's okay to be alone; forever," Rex said.

"You aren't alone, Rex. Everyone finds a companion; even the Jade Rabbit is not alone."

"What do you mean?"

"Your favorite story—the one about the rabbit. Even he wasn't sent up to the moon all alone; he has an eternal companion."

"You didn't tell me the whole story?"

"I did, but there is another story; Chang-e's story."

"Go on."

"Before the beginning of time, a beautiful immortal, Chang'e, lived with her husband, Houyi, happily in heaven. One day the ten sons of the Jade Emperor, the ruler of heaven, were transformed into ten suns, causing the earth to scorch. The Jade Emperor could not stop his sons from destroying the earth, so he asked Houyi, an expert archer, to help him. Houyi shot down and killed nine of the ten suns. Not happy with Houyi's solution, the Emperor banished Houyi and his wife to the earth to live as mortals."

Rex interrupted. "This doesn't sound like a happy story."

"Not all stories are happy, Rex."

"I still want to know what happens."

"All right. Chang'e became sad over the loss of her immortality, so Houyi went on a quest to find an immortality elixir. He went to the Queen Mother of the West who granted him one in the form of a single pill but warned him that he and Chang'e should each only eat one half of the pill to regain their immortality. Houyi returned home and stored the pill in a case. He warned Chang'e not to open the case until they could both share the pill. Then Houyi left the house and Chang'e became curious. She opened the case and—"

"Let me guess, she ate it?"

"Yes, she accidently swallowed the whole pill. As soon as Houyi came home, Chang'e began to float up to the sky. She landed on the moon where she now resides today with her companion, the Jade Rabbit who continues to mix the elixir of life."[5]

"That's sad, though," Rex said. "Houyi lost his wife."

"Yes, and Chang'e lost her husband. It's sad. Life is sad. My point was that the Jade Rabbit is not alone. He has Chang'e."

"The moon is a sad place," Rex said as he closed his eyes to sleep.

Then he heard Mei's loud voice. "Are you sleeping?"

"Not anymore. What's wrong?"

"Everything," Mei said.

"What do you mean?"

"I'm pregnant with Jack's baby."

5   https://en.wikibooks.org/wiki/Chinese_Stories/Houyi_and_Chang%27e; and see https://creativecommons.org/licenses/by-sa/3.0/ (changes made)

Rex was stunned. "Are you all right? Have you talked to a doctor? Why didn't you say anything sooner?"

"I'm fine. I just needed to tell someone. Go back to sleep."

Rex sat up. "Are you serious? How can I sleep now?"

Mei turned her back to him. "I don't want to discuss it."

"But Mei, you'll have to go home."

"I can't."

"Are you going to keep it?"

"Of course I'm going to keep it."

"Then I don't think you have a choice."

"I have time."

"No, Mei, it's not safe. There's no medical care up here."

"We have Lucas," Mei said.

"Like I said, there's no medical care up here."

"He helped you."

"That remains to be seen."

"Well, I'm staying. Goodnight."

Rex tried to continue the conversation, but Mei ignored him. He was perplexed by her sudden revelation, but he decided not to push the topic. It took him over an hour to fall back to sleep. He had many questions and worries for Mei. He figured that she would discuss it in more detail when she was ready. She was probably still in shock.

CHAPTER FOURTEEN

WHILE WAITING FOR the helium-3 extraction process to finish, Rex further analyzed the pallasite meteorite samples from Sverdrup Crater. After he completed his review, he focused on the other rock samples. Most were typical anorthosite rocks. There were, however, a few interesting pieces of green, gold, and black breccia. He examined the breccia rocks under the microscope and gave each of them a number, which he marked on each specimen with a laser pen. He then entered his conclusions into his cataloguing system by describing them out loud so that the computer could record his findings.

Rex rarely took the time to log anything and it was not something the company cared about. However, he took it upon himself to take a few rock samples from each new mining region and classify them. The samples from the crater floor certainly merited this type of analysis. He knew there were many scientists that would be interested in this information, and it could be useful at some time in the future.

Just as Rex picked up a piece of poikilitic breccia, the floor and everything else in the lab shook. He leaned against the table for support, but when it moved and the floor beneath him bounced, Rex lost his balance and fell. The rock samples he had classified and placed in a metal basket for storage also fell to the floor and scattered. The lights flickered for a few seconds and then stabilized. He sat on the floor and waited to get up until he was sure that the shaking was over. There must have been an explosion somewhere on or near the base. Rex looked around the lab at the air vents for smoke but saw none. He got to his feet and limped over to the doorway where he had left his crutch, which was now also lying on the floor. As he lowered his upper body to grab the crutch, he held tightly onto the doorframe. Once upright, he walked out of the room and continued down the hall to see what was going on. As he turned the corner where the fusion lab was located, he spotted Judith.

"Wait up!"

Judith turned to see who was hailing her. She ran over to Rex as he hobbled in her direction. "What happened?"

"I don't know," Rex said. "Let's go find out."

Rex and Judith walked together toward the cafeteria, which had become the de facto meeting place for news.

"What do you think it was?" Judith asked.

"I don't know."

"The Russians?"

"No alarms have gone off," Rex said.

"Not yet."

When they reached the cafeteria, Judith immediately started asking the others if they knew anything. No one had any answers. Mei entered the room with Feng Feng, and they walked over to Rex and Judith, looking for answers to the same questions. Everyone was concerned and had a look of unease about them. Nothing like this had happened on the base before. The last incident, other than the communication blockage, was a few months ago when the lights did not work. It had been due to a faulty solar generator, which Feng Feng was able to repair within a few hours.

Wes walked into the room. Everyone quieted down so that he could speak. Wes stood in the center of the cafeteria and addressed the crowd. "Our communication systems are down again. A Russian ship entered the lunar orbit and destroyed the communications box we set up outside. The ship is currently in orbit, hovering above the base."

The crew posed questions to Wes. They asked him if anyone in the control room had spoken to the Russian ship, whether the Russian ship had sent any warnings, and if there was any threat to the base. Wes explained that he did not have any more information other than that which he had just conveyed. He then made his exit, leaving everyone in the cafeteria to speculate about what was going on.

Judith turned to Rex. "I would have preferred to hear that the base was on fire."

Feng Feng motioned for them to follow him to the lounge. They all walked over to the plasma window.

The four of them got as close to the window as possible, squeezing in next to each other, to see if they could find the ship. A crowd gathered behind them. People were mumbling and trying to peek out the window.

"There it is!" Rex pointed out a bright white artificial light surrounded by several blinking red and green lights hovering above the moon.

The crowd became more vocal, and people were asking unanswerable questions such as "Is it a weapon?" and "Are they going to attack?" and "What do they want?" The most puzzling question for Rex was how a ship that far away could take out a communications box on the base's perimeter. Rex and the others continued to stare out the window until it became clear that the ship was not landing. The four of them stepped back to let the others have a better a look. As they watched and whispered to each other, Dana moved closer to Feng Feng and wrapped her arm around his.

Mei leaned over to Rex and whispered, "I knew she liked him."

Rex nodded. He shifted his attention from outside and watched Feng Feng and Dana interact. Feng Feng always seemed to know the proper etiquette for any situation. Feng Feng took Dana's arm and led her back to a table in the lounge for conversation. Rex recalled Feng Feng's account of his ride up to the base with Dana, and he wondered if this was her way of seeking comfort in scary situations. Rex looked back at the window. Instead of watching the ship, he gazed into the dark empty space that surrounded them and thought about their solitary predicament.

A few hours later, Rex and Mei were having dinner in the cafeteria. Rex stabbed his reconstituted chicken patty with his fork to hold it down while he cut it into squares. Mei had noodles and broth. Rex regretted his meal choice after comparing his food to hers. He was about to take a bite, when there was a loud explosion. The lights flickered. His first thought was that ship was firing on the base. The walls shook. He ducked under the table, grabbed Mei's hands, and pulled her down with him. The shaking quickly subsided.

"We're not really safe down here," Mei said.

"Right. Sorry." Rex said. "I was acting on instinct."

Rex sat back up. "Let's go." He picked up his crutch, and he and Mei walked to the lounge. When they arrived, Feng Feng and Dana were still sitting in the corner together. Feng Feng waved them over to join them.

Dana looked particularly upset. "Are they going to kill us?"

"I think it was just a warning," Feng Feng said.

"Firing on an unarmed base seems like overkill," Mei said.

"Why don't we just open the damned hangar?" Dana asked.

"I imagine we're not allowed," Mei said.

"The company shouldn't be involved in such a mess," Dana said.

"The Russians would not dare provoke the Chinese," Feng Feng said.

"They seem to be doing a pretty good job so far," Dana said.

"They must have a better plan than blowing us all up," Feng Feng said.

Both Dana and Mei looked at Feng Feng with wide eyes. Dana lightly smacked Feng Feng's arm. "Don't even joke."

"We're all thinking it, right?" Feng Feng looked at Rex for support.

"I think this is only the beginning," Rex said.

"We're the least informed and most central to the controversy," Dana said.

Feng Feng grasped Dana's hand. "Cool minds will prevail, I'm sure of it."

Rex was concerned. A bunch of unarmed scientists were certainly not going to keep the Russians out if they were intent on coming in. While they all accepted the innate risks of space travel and living on an experimental moon base, nobody signed up to fight in the first space war.

Ed started to make an announcement to the crew from the intercom system. He did not come down to the cafeteria or send Wes in his place. Everyone became quiet in order to hear.

"The Russian ship has fired a warning shot near the base, which you all recently felt. Nothing was damaged. They've given us a deadline of five days to let them in to do an inspection. Moon-X has denied this request. The Russian Federation has agreed with the Chinese government to assist in the evacuation of all non-essential Chinese personnel from the base. Only those personnel whose names appear on a list to be provided shortly are being evacuated. I will let you know when this list is available. The U.S. government is urging all American personnel to remain and hold their positions on the base. They are working on making arrangements to send a U.S. shuttle later if it can be negotiated. That's all."

The room was abuzz with chatter. Rex could hear the people sitting next to them debating whether the Russians were bluffing, whether they should evacuate, and whether there would be repercussions for evacuating if their name did not appear on the list. Rex did not want to participate in the speculation about who would be leaving.

Rex could see through the plasma window that the Russian ship had moved closer. It was now fully visible and hovering over the moon's surface, facing the base in a menacing fashion. Rex could see the fear in Mei's eyes. Rex and Feng Feng leaned in closer for a better look without getting up.

"Is it going to land?" Dana asked.

"It's just hovering there," Feng Feng said.

"What are they going to do next?" Mei asked.

"We'll be the first to know," Rex said.

"I wish they would go away," Dana said.

They continued to stare at the window, waiting for the ship to move or do something, but it did not. Rex almost wanted the ship to move so there would be something new to talk about. He knew he would have to remain on the base. He wondered whether Mei and Feng Feng were on the evacuation list. He hoped that Mei was on the list, and he knew that even if Feng Feng *were* on the list, he would not leave Dana now. He was afraid for them all.

CHAPTER FIFTEEN

REX STOPPED HIS work in the mining lab to listen to Ed's announcement. The Chinese evacuee list was posted. He went to his monitor on the wall to read the names. Mei's name was on the list; Feng Feng's was not. Rex put his rock samples away and went to find Mei. Luckily, his first stop was her quarters, and she was inside, so there was no need to walk around the base looking for her with his cumbersome crutch. Mei was sitting in the chair next to her bed. She waved for him to come inside.

Rex put down his crutch and sat down on her bed. "What are you going to do?"

"I can't go back," Mei said.

"But you have to."

"Do I?"

Rex put his hand on Mei's shoulder. "It's not safe for you, not now."

"What if I miss the shuttle?"

Rex laughed. "That's not possible; they will be out there waiting a long time."

"Things happen," Mei said.

"Mei, please, there's no reason to be here anymore."

Mei got up and moved over to her desk. "You don't understand. My work is not finished."

"That's not what's important now."

Mei took a stern tone. "It's the only thing that's important now."

"How can you say that?"

"If I leave now, with my work unfinished, I have nothing to offer when I get home. I will have no job, and my family is not going to understand me giving birth to a baby that is not Quon's."

"But Mei, they have to understand that you must move on."

"They will not support me or this child."

"There's no perfect solution, but I am sure a university would take you."

"No, not without a breakthrough," Mei said.

"You don't know that."

"What about you then? I suppose you're all packed?"

Rex did not answer.

"Exactly," Mei said.

"Things will probably get worse up here," Rex said.

"Right," Mei said, "and if I leave now, then whoever continues with my work will get all of the credit when things get better."

"But you have to consider the possibility that Moon-X may walk away from everything," Rex said.

"Not while I'm up here."

Rex said exactly what was on his mind. "If you are planning on keeping Jack's baby, you have to go."

"And if I leave, and something happens up here to everyone, how could I live with that?"

Rex shook his head. "Staying won't prevent that."

"I won't have to live with the knowledge of it, though."

"Better to live," Rex said.

"Is it?"

"Mei! Listen to yourself. You aren't thinking right."

"I can't lose anyone else. Not you, not Feng Feng, not anyone. Not after—" Mei stopped speaking. She turned her head away, trying to hold back her tears and refused to look at or talk to Rex any further. Rex could offer no more rebuttals. He knew there would be no convincing her, other than taking her to the shuttle himself.

"You know what you have to do."

"Leave me alone to think," Mei said.

Rex nodded. Mei stood up and helped Rex get to his feet. Then she went over to her closet and grabbed a bottle of Scotch from a box.

"What's this?"

"It's Jack's. You might as well have it now."

"Are you sure?"

"What am I going to do with it?" Mei was almost pushing him out of her room with the bottle.

"All right, thanks, Mei," Rex said as he turned to leave. He did not want to leave her, but he understood how it felt to want to be alone for a while.

❊

Rex took the Scotch to the lounge. The room was already full when he arrived. Everyone was gathered near the plasma window again. Rex spied Feng Feng and Dana at a table near the window and joined them. Feng Feng moved over so that Rex could see outside. There were five small ships slowly making their way across the surface of the moon, spraying an unknown substance.

"How long has this been going on?" Rex asked.

"It started an hour ago," Feng Feng said.

Rex set the bottle down on the table. "What are they doing?"

"No idea," Dana said.

"Maybe they're making some sort of perimeter around the base," Feng Feng said.

"I hope that's all they're doing," Rex said. He was mesmerized by the activities outside. Feng Feng provided all of the details he knew. "There are more ships, but we can't see them anymore."

"How many?" Rex asked.

"I saw seven," Feng Feng said. He opened the bottle of Scotch and sniffed it. "Shall we?"

"Please," Rex said.

"I'll get some cups," Feng Feng said as he left the table.

"Where did you get this?" Dana asked.

"Mei gave it to me," Rex said. "It's Jack's."

"She didn't want to join us?" Dana asked.

"No."

"Strange," Dana said. "Is she okay?"

"Yes, she just needs to rest." Rex leaned back in an attempt to make his leg more comfortable.

Feng Feng returned with the cups and Dana arranged them as Feng Feng poured everyone a drink.

"I don't think Mei's going to leave," Rex said.

Feng Feng took a sip of his drink. "Maybe she'll change her mind."

Rex wanted to talk to Feng Feng about Mei's situation, but not in front of Dana. He would have to wait and find a better time to discuss the issue with him later. Rex changed the subject. "What about you? They can't make you stay; have you thought about leaving anyway?"

Dana spoke for Feng Feng. "We'll leave when the American shuttle comes to get us."

Rex gulped his drink. "What if there is no American shuttle?"

"Then we stay," Feng Feng said as if there was nothing wrong with staying.

Rex started to believe that none of them would be leaving the base and began to feel the weight of this in his stomach. He did not want to talk anymore, so he drank...a lot.

CHAPTER SIXTEEN

REX COULD NOT sleep. He thought about the ships outside. He sat up and noticed that it was 4:28 a.m. He had been tossing in bed for an hour already. He took his blanket and moved over to his desk. He called out to Pops to give him a visual of what was going on outside of the base. A holographic window appeared in front of him, revealing the activity outside from the vantage point of the plasma window in the lounge. There was a violet glow coming from the direction of the lunar horizon. Rex moved closer to get a better look. The lunar soil was burning.

"Pops, what is that?"

"Your guess is as good as mine," Pops said.

"What is your guess?"

"Looks like they ignited whatever they were spraying out there," Pops said.

"Are they still spraying?"

"Yes."

"But they only ignited one section?"

"Yes."

"So, it's probably a test."

"Maybe," Pops said.

"And they're spraying everywhere?"

"As far as I can see."

Rex became concerned. "Can you get a soil analysis from any of the harvesters?"

"No."

"Why not?"

"I don't have legs."

"We don't have time for this. Can you make contact with the harvesters?"

"If you give me access."

"Yes, access granted."

"Okay, now what?"

"Ask one of the harvesters in the area for a soil analysis. Then tell me what they're spraying."

"Isn't it a bit early for work?"

"If I'm correct, then I'm late."

Rex watched the image of burning ground as he waited for Pops's analysis. The regolith was aflame; but instead of a raging fire, the flames smoldered. Fire behaved differently on the moon. The only source of oxygen for the flames was inside of the soil. The flames formed bubble-shaped domes in lieu of pointy elliptical flames due to the low gravity and lack of oxygen. The movement of the stunted fire created a wavelike effect across the surface of the moon, which undulated like a neon purple ocean.

"All right," Pops said, "you're not going to like this."

"Tell me."

"Magnesium mixed with ammonium nitrate."

"They're spraying flash powder everywhere," Rex said.

"Boom!"

"That's not remotely funny. Do you think they are spraying this over the entire surface?"

"Yes," Pops said. "They have covered a good deal already."

Rex knew that a white-hot magnesium fire, burning at twenty-two hundred degrees Celsius, would easily exceed the necessary temperature of six hundred degrees Celsius to release all gases from the regolith.

"They're burning the helium-3 out of the soil," Rex said.

"Yup."

The Russian ships were destroying the moon's greatest resource. Rex's entire body vibrated with anger. He felt trapped, only being capable of watching the travesty take place.

"Pops, tell the harvesters to dump their cargo and return to the base."

"I'm on it."

Rex sat back in his chair. "I think Mei should get on that shuttle."

"Then put me on it, too," Pops said. "I don't want to go down with the ship."

"You know I can't leave."

"But I can!" Pops said.

"Not without me."

"I'm fine going on my own."

"Not going to happen."

"Why not? Let's pack up and go. I've almost got all of the data about the *Minerva* from the Russian lab now."

"Americans can't leave," Rex said.

"That's silly," Pops said. "Just tell them you're Chinese, and get on the evacuation shuttle."

"That's not going to work," Rex said.

"Why not?"

"I don't have time to explain this to you, Pops."

"Fine," Pops said. "You're welcome."

"Thank you," Rex said.

Rex continued to watch the fire. The light from the burning soil fluctuated in intensity as the gas in the regolith was released. The embers glowed on the horizon like hot coals in stark contrast to the naturally gray lunar dirt. The smoldering light was almost pleasing to look at, but Rex's knowledge of its origin prevented him deriving any pleasure from the scene.

He needed to tell Ed. Rex got up and put on his clothes as quickly as he could. He grabbed his crutch and made his way toward the control room. The hall was quiet. Rex imagined that people were either still sleeping or watching the activity outside of the base on their monitors, too afraid to come out.

When Rex reached the control room, Ed was not there. Wes was working in his place again.

"Where's Ed?" Rex hoped that he was not asleep in his quarters. He had already determined not to go to Ed's quarters again if he could help it.

"He went to the hangar to inspect the doors," Wes said. "He doesn't want to be disturbed."

Rex found this peculiar since Ed could have sent anyone to check the doors. "Are you watching what's going on outside?"

"Yes," Wes said.

"Is the military going to do anything?"

"I don't know," Wes said.

"Is there anything we can do?"

"I'm open to suggestions."

"What if we just let them in like they want?"

"I'd be out of a job."

"What's more important at this point?" Rex asked.

"I wish it were up to me," Wes said.

Rex left the room and headed to the hangar. When he entered the hangar it was dimly lit and the automatic lights did not turn on. Rex had to squint his eyes to see. He heard clanging noises coming from the far left-hand corner. He shouted out to Ed so as not to completely surprise him. Ed peered up from a large rectangular piece metal that he was holding.

"Don't come any closer," Ed said.

Rex stopped in his tracks. "What's going on, Ed?"

"What are you doing here, Rex?"

"I came to find you."

"What do you want?"

"I want to talk."

"Find me later, I'm busy."

"This can't wait," Rex said.

"Go back, Rex. I said I'm busy right now."

"What are you doing in here, Ed?"

"Nothing that concerns you."

Rex stepped closer.

"Stop!" Ed shouted more urgently.

Rex disregarded his warnings and stepped closer and closer to Ed, who now dropped the piece of metal he held. The metal landed on the floor with a resounding thud, which echoed through the empty hangar. Rex halted his advance momentarily.

"What are you doing?"

"I told you, I'll talk to you later." Ed fumbled around, trying to push a box behind him.

Rex saw that Ed was standing in front of a pit in the floor, and the metal that he was holding was its cover.

"What are you hiding there?" Rex asked.

"Get out, Rex."

"Seriously, what's going on?"

"I said get out!" Ed was shouting at full volume.

Rex was now only a few feet away from Ed. As Rex took another step closer, Ed lunged at him and pushed him backward, causing him to drop his crutch and lose his footing. He fell to the floor.

"What the hell?" Rex shouted.

"I told you to leave."

Rex saw three cylindrical metal devices in the pit behind Ed. He instantly recognized them as nuclear devices. "Whatcha' got there, Ed?"

Ed paused for a moment to catch his breath. He exhaled slowly as he spoke. "You need to leave, and forget about anything you think you might have seen here."

"Are you planning on using those?"

Ed did not respond. He stared at Rex and shook his head back and forth a few times. After he felt comfortable that Ed was not going to push him down again, Rex stood up.

"Get out, Rex."

"If you're planning on using those, we have a right to know."

Ed got in Rex's face. "We can't use what we don't have."

Rex now understood everything. "So that's what's in that bunker in the crater."

Ed said nothing.

Rex continued his questioning of Ed. "Why are those inside the base then?"

"Dammit, Rex! This isn't your concern."

"Damn right it's my concern! I have a right to know if what the Russians are saying is true! They're blaming my work anyway."

Ed looked at Rex with disdain.

Rex matched his stare. "I'm not leaving until you explain."

Ed stopped trying to get Rex to leave. "We didn't have time to move them to the bunker before that ship started hovering, and then the other ships came."

"But how?"

Ed waited for Rex to figure it out.

"Jack?"

Ed took a step back. "Who else?"

"Did he know what he was flying with?"

"Of course."

"Now what? You can't possibly let the Russians in here."

"That's right."

"Is the government sending anyone to help?" Rex asked.

"They don't want to escalate the situation."

"Then what are we going to do?"

"We're going to sit tight," Ed said.

"And where are you moving them now?"

"I'm trying to get them outside of the base."

"But they're watching everything."

"We can go out to check on the harvesters, and they won't suspect that we are actually moving something."

"I just parked the harvesters," Rex said.

"Why?"

"Do you know what they're doing out there? They're spraying flash powder all over the soil and burning it. The harvesters are mining aluminum nitrate," Rex said.

"I didn't know."

"What did you think they were doing?"

"I thought they were going to try to smoke us out, so they could get inside."

"It's worse than that," Rex said. "They're incinerating all of the helium-3—all of it!"

Ed stepped back and put the lid back over the hole in the floor. "I better leave these here, then."

"Only if you think the base is safe," Rex said.

"It is for now."

"You shouldn't have allowed this, Ed. You've put us all in danger." Having nothing more to ask of Ed, he turned around and limped toward the door.

"Forget you were here!" Ed shouted after him.

"I wish I could!" Rex shouted back into the darkness as he walked to the door. He was enraged. Before exiting, Rex turned back around. "I quit! Tell Hendricks I'm finished!"

❈

The confirmation of Rex's suspicions about what was being stored in Sver-drup Crater was alarming. The crew was in much greater danger than they knew. What was even worse was that the company deliberately misled them. Moon-X denied being partial to any one of their shareholders. Nonetheless, they allowed the Americans to expel the Russians and hide nuclear weapons. Placing nuclear weapons on the moon was a violation of the Moon Treaty. Rex had always been sensitive about the politics of his work; however, he never let himself fully believe that it was totally a political endeavor. Now he could not escape that conclusion.

Rex believed in the original mission of the company. Now it seemed that his work was only meant to provide a cover for the military. His legs became weak. He slowed his pace and rested in the hall for moment. His throat was dry and his hands were clammy. Rex was angry with Ed and Hendricks. He considered leaving with Mei on the evacuation shuttle, but he knew that if he left, the government might misconstrue his actions. Now that he wanted to leave, he could not. The only other person on the base to whom he could confide the information about the weapons was Feng Feng.

Rex caught his breath and made his way down to the track to find Feng Feng. It was 6:00 a.m., and Feng Feng was usually up and exercising by this time. Rex stepped onto the track. He heard someone running and he presumed it was Feng Feng so he walked down the track to meet him. As soon as he saw Feng Feng he waved him over.

Rex turned around and walked with Feng Feng. "I just saw Ed in the hangar."

"What was he doing in there so early?"

"Remember that door we found down in the crater?"

Feng Feng shook his head. "I don't want to hear this, Rex. I didn't see anything in the crater."

"I know you did," Rex said.

"No," Feng Feng said, "I didn't."

"I get it, but now I know for sure what's in there."

"I don't want to hear this, Rex."

"You need to know."

"No, I don't, and it doesn't make any difference what I know or don't know. There's nothing we can do about it."

"Just listen."

"Do you know what happens to troublemakers in my country?"

"I have a good idea," Rex said.

"No, you don't know the half of it, and I have parents who need me."

"Yes, and if you want to get home to them, you'd better listen," Rex said. "We're all in danger. Jack brought nukes up here."

Feng Feng's brow wrinkled up, showing concern. "Are you sure?"

"I saw them. I walked in on Ed moving them. Jack was transporting them, and Ed was hiding them in the crater. But now with the Russians watching, Ed can't move them."

"The Russians are right, then," Feng Feng said.

Rex nodded. "You and Dana should leave on that shuttle."

"I can't."

"Why?"

"I was told to stay," Feng Feng said. "I have to work on the solar panels; and with everyone else leaving, they need me to stay."

"Can't you work something out?"

"Are you going?" Feng Feng asked.

"I can't," Rex said.

"See?"

"I know," Rex said, "but this is getting scary. The Russians aren't going to give up their campaign outside, and the U.S. military isn't going to allow Ed to let them in, especially with you-know-what's lying around."

"They are going to force their way in," Feng Feng said.

"If they do, Ed will fight, and that means the base gets destroyed."

"Then let's hope I'm wrong."

Rex looked at Feng Feng. "We have to get Mei on that shuttle at least."

"Why?" Feng Feng asked. "Even if we tell her, she won't go."

Rex took a deep breath and slowed his pace. "Mei's pregnant."

Feng Feng stopped walking. "What?"

"I know, it's hard to believe, but she told me. Didn't you notice how she wasn't drinking in the lounge anymore?"

"I didn't think much of it," Feng Feng said.

"Well, we all know you've been busy." Rex nudged Feng Feng.

"It's Jack's, right?"

"Yes," Rex said.

Feng Feng moved forward again at a slow pace. "And she plans on keeping it?"

"Yes, and I don't understand why she isn't ready to leave already."

"Rex, she will have to explain her condition to her family, and Quon's family."

"But they don't have to know."

Feng Feng scoffed. "Mei and Quon lived with his parents."

"They can't expect her to mourn forever."

"No, but they haven't seen her since she and Quon left for the moon base."

"But it's not safe for her here, not just because of the nukes. There's no doctor on the base, and Lucas is barely qualified to administer a saline drip."

"I agree with you completely."

"What can we do to get her on that shuttle?"

"We will have to trick her," Feng Feng said.

"How?"

"We must pretend to go with her. Get her to the shuttle and turn around."

"You think we can do that?"

"Why not?"

"I don't know if Mei will believe me that I'm leaving, even though I quit."

"Quit?"

"Yes, I told Ed that I quit as I left the hangar."

"Go back and tell Ed you didn't mean it."

Rex shook his head. "I meant it. I don't see how I can keep working after this."

"It's about the science, not the company."

"I can't go on with it, not now."

"Reconsider, scientists have always been used by the military in some way. I still think your fusion project is legitimate."

"I'll think about it."

"Yes, think hard. In the meantime, let's get Mei out of here," Feng Feng said.

Rex and Feng Feng continued discussing the details of the plan as they finished a lap. Feng Feng would agree not to tell Mei about the weapons. He was adamant that having such knowledge would only put Mei in a more precarious position. They concurred that the only way she would go is if they both left with her. Despite Feng Feng's acknowledgement of the danger facing them, he was adamant about staying on as ordered, especially since Dana was staying. They discussed getting her on the shuttle as well, but they could not agree whether to tell her about the nuclear weapons. After a lengthy debate, they decided that it would unethical to tell Dana and not everyone else. They agreed, however, to let Dana in on their plan to get Mei to leave and ask her to participate. Rex knew that Mei would be angry with him for not getting on the shuttle with her. He determined, however, that it was more important for her to be safe. Unlike the rest of the crew, Mei had a medical issue. Even in the best-case scenario where the political maelstrom blew over, Mei would still need to leave the base. Rex and Feng Feng finished formulating their plan and then parted ways to go about their day.

CHAPTER SEVENTEEN

REX SAT IN the lounge, looking out at the Russian ship hovering near the base. He wondered what the people inside were doing and what they were thinking. The threatening posture of the ship could only lead one to believe that the pilot had ill intentions. Three evacuation shuttles had already left this afternoon, taking twenty-two Chinese nationals to the Russian space station. There were two more scheduled and then no more. The last shuttle was scheduled to leave soon. The base was already quieter in every corridor except on the Chinese side, where there had been a constant stream of farewell get-togethers. Rex attended a few of these gatherings earlier in the day, but he left to gather his thoughts and prepare himself for getting Mei on the last shuttle.

As he watched the ship, his doubts faded about whether or not they were doing the right thing. Now he had to put on a good act to get Mei to go along. Rex stood up. He needed to pack a small bag to take with him, when they went to fetch Mei, to make his plea to leave more convincing. He walked slowly, leaning on his crutch, back to his quarters. Before exiting, he looked back at the empty lounge and remembered how it used to be full of tired but hopeful scientists when they first arrived on the base. Everyone was boisterous and eager to meet each other. Later, people gravitated to people in their own fields, and many only associated with their own nationals, especially after the *Minerva* was lost. Now social interactions were focused on information gathering and comfort seeking.

Rex said goodbye to many people earlier in the day—many he barely knew and whose absence should not have really bothered him, but it did.

In the corridor leading to his quarters, he overhead comments from the remaining crew. They were sure that everything would blow over in a few weeks and that new scientists would come. Rex thought they sounded naïve and he was sorry that they were so misled. The mission was falling apart, and it seemed more likely that the entire base would be abandoned. He walked faster, which made his knee hurt more. At first he was able to ignore it, but by the time he arrived at his quarters, he needed to sit down, raise his leg, and massage around the knee to alleviate the throbbing.

Rex looked around and thought about what he would take if he really were leaving. He did not have much time before he had to meet Feng Feng. Rex hobbled over to his closet to find the small black bag that he had come with. They had all been given identical duffel bags to travel with. It was still resting on the shelf where he originally put it. He imagined he would be taking that bag home under much different circumstances. Rex removed an extra blanket he had on a shelf in his closet and threw it in the bag. He examined the bag to see if the blanket made it look stuffed enough. It did not, so he took a pair of black pants and black shirt from his stack of uniforms and threw them in his bag. He examined the bag again, touching it on both sides to see if the extra garments made it look full. He was satisfied. Next he walked over to his desk and took some of the pallasite meteorite samples from the crater that Mei liked and added them to his bag. He thought they would make a nice gift for her. He held up his picture of Avery that was sitting on his desk and looked at it. He wondered what she would have said about all of this. He put the picture back down in its original spot.

Rex sat down at his desk and started looking for a piece of paper to write on. It was his intention to leave his bag with Mei and enclose a note explaining why he and Feng Feng had tricked her into getting on the shuttle. He tried to write a heartfelt note, but he could not clear his thoughts well enough to express them on paper. Instead, he grabbed the anthology of Chinese poetry that Mei gave to him. He flipped through the book and stopped on the page with Li Bai's "Seeing a Friend Off." Rex slowly re-read the poem. He tore out the page and placed it inside of his bag. He hoped that Mei would find it later.

Through the monitor in his quarters Rex watched the last Russian shuttle land. It maneuvered into position to take aboard its final group of passengers. The shuttle resembled an American shuttle except that it was shorter, not to mention that it was older and looked more used with paint scratches and dents. There did not appear to be any movement yet from within the ship. After he got what he felt to be a satisfactory look at the shuttle, he decided it was time to meet Feng Feng and Dana and fetch Mei. Rex retrieved Pops and put him behind his ear in case he needed him.

CHAPTER EIGHTEEN

WITH SINGLE-MINDED PURPOSE, Rex zipped up his bag, threw it over his right shoulder, and proceeded down the corridor while supporting himself with his crutch under his left arm. The hall was empty. The farewell gatherings had dispersed, and the remaining scientists had retreated to their quarters or their workstations. He only had to make it down one more corridor before he arrived at Mei's door. He was sure that she would be there at this time, but for a moment Rex feared that she might be elsewhere on the base. He and Feng Feng agreed to wait until the last minute to approach her to get her on the last shuttle; but if they had to take time to go find her, it could muck up their plan completely.

As Rex turned the corner and arrived at Mei's quarters, Feng Feng poked his head out of Mei's door and motioned for Rex to hurry up. Rex was relieved. He entered the room and Feng Feng moved over to the desk to make space for him. Two bags, presumably Feng Feng's and Dana's, were lying on the floor. They were identical to the one Rex was carrying.

Mei looked distraught. Her brow was furrowed and her cheeks were flushed. She turned to Rex. "I'm not leaving." Rex looked to Feng Feng for assistance, but Feng Feng only motioned with his eyes as if to say that Rex needed to persuade her.

Rex dropped his bag and put his hand on Mei's left shoulder. "We have to get out of here. Sergei sent me a message that the Russians are going to force their way into the base."

Mei moved away from Rex. "How can you be sure?"

"I'm not, but do you want to take the chance?"

"Shouldn't you warn Ed?"

Rex hesitated for a moment. He hated lying to Mei. His throat dried up and his voice was raspy, yet he pressed on. "I did."

"And?"

"I told him, and he didn't take me seriously."

"What did he say about the warning that the Russians would break in?"

"He said it would happen over his dead body," Rex said.

"He'll be the death of us all."

"We have to go, Mei. I don't like it either, but sometimes you have to put yourself first."

"You're really going?"

"We're all going," Feng Feng said.

"I don't know," Mei said.

"We have to go now," Dana said.

Mei defiantly turned her head away from Rex. He knew they had little time and became frustrated. "Dammit, Mei, it's not safe in your condition!"

"My condition!" Mei shrieked. "You told them?"

Rex did not respond.

"How could you?" Mei pushed Rex.

Rex grabbed Mei's hand. "It's not safe here; we're all leaving."

Mei took a step back, forcefully removing her hand from Rex's. She muttered a few words in Mandarin to Feng Feng that Rex did not understand. Then Feng Feng said something back to her. Mei nodded and Rex took this to mean that Mei was going along with their plan.

Dana stood up and walked over to Mei's closet. She opened the door, revealing several uniforms neatly hung side by side. Dana moved the clothes to one side, in search of Mei's tote bag. She found it on the closet floor and placed it in the middle of the room. "I'll help you get your things together."

Mei walked over to the closet to stop her. "No, I don't want anything. I don't want any of it." Dana grabbed some of Mei's clothes and put them in the bag despite what Mei had said. She then handed it to Mei, who did not object to taking it. Feng Feng picked up his and Dana's bags and quickly ushered everyone out of Mei's quarters.

They walked together to the airlock. When they reached the changing room, Rex was pleased that they had timed their exit so well. All of the environmental suits had been returned and were ready to go for the next group of people leaving. Ed would not let the shuttle dock in the hangar, so it had to load everyone outside, necessitating the use of the environmental suits. They all had been made aware of the evacuation procedure. Evacuees were to exit the base and walk to the waiting shuttle. Then they were to check in with the Russians. Once inside the shuttle, their suits would be returned to the base by Wes, who was in charge of managing the evacuation process.

Everyone suited up. As Mei turned around to pick up her helmet, which was sitting on the bench behind her, Rex swapped his bag for hers. He was about put on his helmet when Mei stopped him. Rex froze.

"Are you sure about this?" Mei asked.

"Yes," Rex said before quickly putting on his helmet. He was the first one fully suited. His environmental suit was heavy and hard to move in while inside. It was also warm and Rex was already perspiring. Mei watched Dana and Feng Feng put on their helmets before fastening hers. Once everyone was ready, they moved into the airlock. Feng Feng gave the go signal with his hand. Everyone checked their suits one last time and gave him the thumbs-up. They did not sync their communicators because this was not a working mission. Also, Rex did not want to field any more questions from Mei. As soon as he was ready to go, he called out to Pops.

"I want you to be quiet now."

"I wasn't talking," Pops said.

"I know, but I need you to be quiet until we get back to the base."

"Why?"

"We're going for a walk," Rex said. "I'll explain later."

"You're welcome."

"Thank you," Rex said.

Feng Feng opened the airlock and exited first, holding the door for everyone else to pass through. Rex was the last one out. The shuttle was six hundred meters away. Wes waited on the LRV by the shuttle to return their suits back to the base. Mei, Dana, and Feng Feng walked together at the same pace. Rex followed behind them because of his knee and lack of a crutch. The lower gravity made it easier for him to walk, but his knee did not bend properly, making it difficult for Rex to steady himself as he bounced forward toward the shuttle. As they drew near, Rex's perspiration was causing his mask to fog. He asked Pops to adjust the temperature, but he did not respond.

Two Russian soldiers exited the shuttle to greet them. Their bulky lead-gray suits almost worked as moon camouflage, blending in with the landscape. They wore an older-model environmental suit without the nanotechnology developed by the company. Rex knew that they could only wear these suits for thirty-minute intervals, which meant that the soldiers were waiting in the airlock for evacuees to approach the shuttle before coming out. One soldier held an ultrasonic scanner. Rex recognized the scanner because it used the same technology that the company used to identify individual scientists when they arrived on the base. The Russians were apparently still using some of Moon-X's equipment. The other, slightly taller soldier wore a dark-tinted visor that obscured his face. Wes watched them from his LRV. He looked bored and sat with his arm slumped over the steering wheel and head tilted over in the same downward direction, but he perked up when he saw them approach.

Upon reaching the shuttle, one of the Russian soldiers faced them and held up his palm, directing them to stop. The other soldier pointed to a spot on the ground where he wanted them to line up side by side. The soldier holding the scanner grabbed each of their hands, one by one, and waved the scanner over their palms to check them in. Rex was concerned about being identified but did not resist the scan. The soldiers seemed to be at ease with the situation. Rex anticipated more hostility on their part, but there had been none so far.

Rex's mouth was dry, but his arms and back were moist with sweat. He watched Feng Feng closely to see when he would move to pull away. Once the scanning was completed, the tall soldier opened the airlock to the shuttle and motioned for them to enter. Feng Feng stepped back, allowing Mei to go first. His gesture was natural since Feng Feng was so well-mannered and one would expect nothing less. Mei proceeded toward the shuttle and stepped inside. At that moment, Feng Feng tapped Dana and they both abruptly turned in the opposite direction and leapt back toward the base as fast as they could. They ran side by side, Feng Feng making sure he did not get ahead of Dana.

Rex took a breath and turned around. He followed Feng Feng and Dana's lead and leaped after them. He did not look back to see the Russians' reactions. Out of the fear of being pursued, he pushed himself to run as fast as one can run on the surface of the moon. Rex kept his eyes on Feng Feng and Dana, but his helmet visor was foggy, and he could not see the terrain in front of him well. He jumped up and landed on an uneven patch of ground. His right foot landed in a depression and his left on a small mound. A sharp pain ran up his leg, momentarily paralyzing him. His torso continued moving forward while his right leg remained motionless, causing him to fall forward in slow motion. Rex tried to correct the situation by throwing his arms upward, but this only had the effect of making him land on his bad knee. He hit the dirt and bounced.

Feng Feng and Dana kept running and did not look back. Rex saw that they were now at least two hundred meters ahead of him. He pushed himself up as fast as he could. He stood up, but his knee failed him and he stumbled. This time he did not hit the ground; he felt a hand grab him from behind and throw him backward. He landed flat on his back. Confused, Rex pushed himself backward with his legs like a four-legged spider. The tall Russian soldier stood over him. Rex moved to the side, and the soldier moved to block him. The soldier's posture was now more aggressive than it had been minutes before. He motioned for Rex to stop, and when Rex continued to struggle to stand up, the tall soldier quickly used his boot to push him back down. He felt two hands pressing down on his shoulders from behind. The second soldier had caught up with him. Rex was trapped. He called out to Pops, "Couldn't you have warned me?"

"You told me to be quiet," Pops said.

"You can warn me if someone is about to hit me!"

Rex tried to think of ways to outmaneuver the soldiers. He slunk down to evade their hands and, once free of them, rolled to the right, but they pursued. As he spun around, he felt the weight of one of their legs on the back of his suit; it was cutting off his air supply. Rex struggled to escape, but the soldier dropped to his knee, putting more force on Rex's back and preventing him from moving anything but his arms and legs.

Rex dug deep enough into the regolith to push himself forward, but to no avail. He only managed to stir up dust around them. The weight of the soldier on Rex's back diminished Rex's air supply. Rex gasped. "Pops, pump up the oxygen!" He became light-headed. Without a steady supply of oxygen, his helmet only had thirty seconds' worth of breathable air. The soldier pushed down harder on his back. Rex stopped struggling and played possum in hopes that the soldier would ease up. Luckily, he did not have to wait long. The weight on top of him eased and his oxygen flowed again.

"Where are they now, Pops?" A red light appeared in the corner of his visor.

Rex turned over and sat up. He saw Wes and the tall soldier wrestling each other on the ground. Rex stood up and ran toward Wes to help.

"Look out!" Pops said.

Before Rex could react, the other Russian soldier pushed Rex. He fell to the ground, knocking his helmet on a rock.

"Pops, can you contact the base for help?"

Pops's voice gurgled something indistinguishable back. The blow damaged the audio components of Rex's helmet. Then, Rex saw the tall soldier pin Wes to the ground and repeatedly punch his visor. Wes's visor finally cracked after several hard blows. The tall soldier stood over Wes, watching him suffocate. Rex cried out to Pops again, but there was still no response. He ran as fast as he could toward Wes, bouncing higher, trying to move forward faster and farther. But before he could reach them, the second soldier appeared on his left side and shoved him. Rex's legs faltered and he began to fall, but he managed to stabilize himself in time. When the second soldier presented himself again, Rex kicked him, and the soldier bounced backward a pace. From this vantage point, Rex watched Dana step inside the base; Feng Feng stood at the entrance, looking back. Rex raised his right arm and moved it back and forth as if he were throwing a baseball, trying to communicate to Feng Feng that he should go inside. This, however, had the opposite effect. Feng Feng ran toward Rex. Rex re-engaged the second Russian soldier who quickly changed his strategy. The soldier crouched down and charged him like an enraged bull. Rex held up his arms to block him; however, the soldier dipped lower and wrapped his arms around Rex's waist and lifted him up by the rib cage, raising him up above his head. Rex found himself facing upward toward outer space. The soldier carried him above his head, holding his neck and right thigh. Rex squirmed and thrashed about, but could not reach any part of the soldier holding him. He was like a bug turned on its back, frantically moving its legs to right itself. Rex made one last desperate attempt to move every muscle in his body at the same time to free himself, but it was of no use.

The soldier reached the shuttle and lowered Rex back down to the ground, shoving him into the airlock. Both soldiers stepped inside. The taller soldier quickly locked the door. The struggle was over. Rex was trapped. He thought about Wes. He screamed from inside his helmet, "Don't leave him!" but no one could hear. He waited with the soldiers as the room filled with air. When the airlock lights turned green, the soldiers removed their helmets, revealing the shorter one's curly blonde hair and the partially bald head of the taller one who had killed Wes. Rex did not take off his helmet. Instead, he took the opportunity to reengage in the fight with them. As the taller one unsnapped his gloves, Rex managed to head-butt him and push him against the wall. He then turned and swung his fist at the other soldier's cheek. The door to the interior of the shuttle swung open, and a young lanky man dressed in a green officer's uniform peeked inside to see what was going on.

Each of the two soldiers grabbed one of Rex's arms and pushed him out of the airlock into the ship. Rex looked around for Mei, but his visor was still foggy and he could not see clearly. The officer stood directly in front of Rex, staring him in the eye, and—in perfect English—ordered him to remove his helmet. Rex was not intimidated by the young officer, but he obeyed. The two soldiers maintained their grip on him. The officer looked to be no more than twenty years old with a beardless face and light-brown spikey hair. The entryway was narrow and rectangular-shaped with storage lockers on either side. Everything looked as if it was painted light gray but in fact was unpainted and merely had been left in its naturally drab state.

"Let me go!" Rex shouted.

The officer gave a command in Russian, directed at the soldiers, and they unhanded Rex.

The officer looked at Rex, confused. "Why did you leave the base?"

"I was escorting my friend onto the shuttle," Rex said. "Now let me go."

He shook his head. "I have orders."

"Orders to kidnap?"

"To evacuate."

Rex's blood boiled with anger. "Let me go, or you'll have to kill me, too!" He turned to the two soldiers and shouted, "Murderers!" He lunged at the tall soldier who was now fully unsuited and therefore able to out-maneuver Rex. The soldier moved to the side and used his knee to trip Rex. He fell to the ground. The soldier dropped down and held him on the floor. Rex struggled, while the officer grabbed an iron rod from inside one of the lockers.

"Believe me," the officer said, "you don't want to be left here." He struck Rex on the head with the rod.

THE
SPACE STATION

CHAPTER NINETEEN

HEN REX AWOKE, he was lying on a small cot against a cold anodized aluminum wall. He was still wearing his environmental suit, but his helmet and gloves sat on an empty cot next to him. He could tell he was in the Russian space station's infirmary, due to all of the scanners and medical equipment around him.

In order to not draw attention to himself, Rex kept as still as possible while observing his surroundings to determine if he was safe. There was a stainless steel procedure table in the middle of the room with medical tools under it. The sidewall was lined with cabinets for medical supplies. There were also miscellaneous medical devices and equipment strewn about on the countertop, such as equipment sterilizers, oxygen tanks, an emergency defibrillator, a portable electrocardiograph machine, an ultrasound machine, a microscope, and a centrifuge. The Russian infirmary was much better stocked than the one on the moon base. An older man leaned on the counter. Rex assumed he was a doctor. The man was tall with a dark complexion, and his face had the wrinkles of a learned man. He resembled a 1950s film star with a dimpled chin, an oval-shaped face, and a full head of naturally coiffed hair.

As soon as Rex locked eyes with the doctor, the doctor approached him. He stood next to Rex and grabbed his wrist to feel his pulse. "How you feeling?" The doctor spoke English with a Russian accent. He held his wrist while he waited for Rex's response.

"Fine."

"No headache?"

Rex's head throbbed, but he had been distracted by his examination of the room so he did not mention it until the doctor asked. "Yes, a little."

The doctor walked over to the side cabinet and removed a bottle of pills. He opened it and put two capsules in his hand. Then he poured a small glass of water from a thermos sitting on the countertop. He walked back over to Rex and handed him the water and pills. Rex sat up and looked at the pills. "What are these?"

"Pain medicine for head. You have nice-sized lump there."

Rex put the pills in his mouth and drank a sip of water. He felt the back of his head to find the lump. The area was sore. He rubbed around the swelling to estimate its circumference. It was about the size of an egg. Rex was apprehensive about what to expect on the Russian station. He wanted more information, so he kept the conversation going. Rex thanked the doctor and introduced himself, but the doctor was already aware of his identity and nationality. The doctor had a calm demeanor and this put Rex more at ease.

"I'm Dr. Ahmyetgali Otkupshchikov. Call me Doctor Gali. I have a difficult name, even for Russians."

"That is quite a name."

"Yes, my father was Russian and my mother was Volga Tatar. Since my father gave me my last name, she wanted to give me a first name that would let everyone know that her son was Tatar."

Rex was not interested in the doctor's background, but he feigned interest, hoping to ingratiate himself with the doctor long enough to obtain some more useful information about the station and what the Russians were planning to do with him.

"Are you from Tartarstan?" he asked.

"Yes, originally from Kazan," Dr. Gali said. "Then I did my studies in Moskva years ago."

"How did you end up here?"

"As they say, long story. It all comes down to politics."

"How so?"

The doctor leaned against the steel table behind him and folded his arms. "My grandfather was high ranking in the Soviet army. I forget what position—commander or division commander. He was positioned in

Tartarstan in the 1920s during the terror famine. One of his tasks was the Sovietization of the region. So, my father grew up in Tartarstan. Eventually, a young Tatar village girl caught his eye. She was youngest daughter of large peasant family. When my father asked for her hand in marriage, they could hardly refuse—especially with the ongoing Russification, and my grandfather being who he was. And so it was, and here I am."

"But how did that lead to your being here on the space station?"

Dr. Gali smiled. "Tides turn, as they say. My mother's family was very large, lots of cousins. After the Soviet Union collapsed, the region was all about de-Russification. My mother's family got involved in state council, and then my younger cousin became council chairman. Now, with the President in need of the support of the republics, he made a gesture of goodwill by sending a Tatar doctor into space. Makes good politics."

"I see. And this is something you wanted to do?"

"Why not? Maybe I can write a good book about my experience when I retire. What about you? Why are you here?"

"I didn't intend to be," Rex said. "I was trying to help a friend."

"No good deed goes unpunished, as you Americans say."

"Right. Now I'm here with a lump on my head."

"Yes." Dr. Gali nodded. "How did that happen?"

"Isn't it obvious?"

Dr. Gali shook his head. "*Nyet.*"

"An officer on the shuttle hit me and knocked me out to prevent me from leaving."

"Ah, that would explain it."

Rex hoped that Dr. Gali could give him some idea about how he might be treated on the station. "How are things here on the station—I mean, with the evacuees?"

"Most have been sent back home already, but not the last shuttle today. There is delay. I don't know why."

"Is there room for everyone up here?" Rex asked.

"Not really, but we will make do. We have a small lounge upstairs where people are gathering."

"Are the shuttles landing in China?"

"*Nyet.* Our President wants to use the new Russian spaceport. He spent much money to construct it; he needs to make it look useful. He says close enough."

Rex grimaced. The doctor noticed.

"What's the matter?" Dr. Gali asked. "Don't you want a free trip to Vostochny?"

"Are there any more shuttles back to the base?"

"No, you were last one."

"What about those other ships working on the moon? Do they come back here?"

The doctor shook his head. "*Nyet.* They stay with the big ship now."

"Do you know what that ship is doing there?"

"Military personnel do not discuss such things with me. They stick to themselves. You will see."

Rex was also curious about what the doctor thought about the situation on the moon. "Do you get much news up here?"

"*Da.* We have access to all world news."

"Our communications were blocked on the base, as you probably know. What have you heard about what's going on?"

The doctor took a deep breath and rubbed his eyes. "What a mess. My government is not happy about being kicked out of the moon base and yours is not happy about the blockade."

"What do you think is going to happen?" Rex asked.

"The soldiers will take over the moon base. I don't know what happens then. What do you think your government will do?"

"I don't know how the government will respond," Rex said, "but I know that the base commander is prepared to fight, even at the risk of destroying the whole base."

"That would be foolish," Dr. Gali said. "They can't fight Russian soldiers."

Rex shrugged. "The commander is ready to go down with his ship."

"Then we are on the verge of war."

"So it seems." Rex wondered if the doctor was being straight with him, but all of his answers sounded plausible enough; besides, Rex would be able to figure the situation out soon enough for himself. "Are we enemies, or am I still allowed to walk around the station?"

The doctor laughed. "No enemies here."

"Prisoner, then?"

The doctor laughed louder. "Where would we keep you? We barely have a enough room for the staff."

"So I am free to wander around?"

"Of course. Most of the interesting places are upstairs. Take a left when you leave."

Rex was surprised that there was no one there to detain or question him. "There are no soldiers to watch over me?"

"I don't see any, do you?"

"I can go?"

"Unless you feel unwell," Dr. Gali said.

Rex stood up. His knee pained him again. He stretched it out in front of him and moved it around a little.

"Is your leg okay? Did you hurt something else?"

"Yes," Rex said, "but it was a while ago."

"Would you like me to take a look at it?"

Rex was eager to go and find Mei, but he also knew that a real doctor had not yet examined his leg, and it might be a while until he got home. "Yes, if you don't mind." Rex removed his suit in order for the doctor to see the full extent of his knee injury. The doctor set Rex's suit on the cot containing the gloves and helmet. Rex sat back down and stuck his leg out for the doctor to examine. Dr. Gali touched the inflamed incision where Lucas had operated.

"You had an operation?"

Rex nodded. "Yes, I fell while—" Rex stopped talking. He realized that he probably should not discuss his suit or the technology in it. He thought it best to not reveal any details about the nanobots, so he changed his story. "I fell and cut myself on broken glass, and our medical technician took care of it."

"Curious. Can you bend your knee?"

"Not well."

The doctor turned and walked over to the countertop. He returned with a handheld ultrasound scanner and waved it over Rex's knee and leg. He walked over to a computer screen to review the results. He studied them silently, flipping back and forth between several images.

Rex grew concerned. "You're worrying me, doc. What do you see?"

Dr. Gali looked up. "Your knee isn't healing well."

"Is there anything you can do for it?"

Dr. Gali reached into the cupboard above him and took out a bottle filled with silver capsules. He removed three of them and plugged a wire into each one. The wires were connected to his computer where he proceeded to program the pills. He then unplugged the capsules, walked back over to Rex, and handed them to him.

"Take these."

"What are they?"

"Mini-surgeons."

Rex was confused. "What do you mean?"

"This is my hobby. In my spare time I make medical devices. I took some microscopic cameras used for surgery and added nanotechnology. These pills will automatically release enzymes that will dissolve the scar tissue in your knee."

"That's brilliant! And they'll do this for me?"

"*Da.*"

Rex swallowed the capsules and waited for something to happen. "I don't feel anything."

"You won't. My nanodocs also release pain medicine."

"Nice."

Dr. Gali went to his closet. "Here are some clean clothes." The uniforms on the station were similar to the company's uniforms but were gray instead of black. Rex got dressed as Dr. Gali cleaned up his workstation. Although the shirt was larger and not as form fitting as the company's uniform, Rex found the new clothes to be more comfortable. Rex was appreciative for the doctor's help but was also wary of leaving his suit behind with him. He was concerned that Dr. Gali might try to reverse-engineer it, but from what he saw, the doctor's knowledge was likely more advanced than what was in the suit.

"How long until I can go?" Rex asked.

"You can go anytime."

"Thank you for your help."

"Sure. Come back if you have any more trouble; I'm always here."

"Good, I'll come back to retrieve my suit later."

"No need. I will hang it up. I don't think you will be needing it for a while."

Rex hesitated, but decided he could not haul the suit around with him anyway. He stood up to leave. He did not feel any tightness or pain in his leg. He shook it a few times. It felt completely normal. "Amazing." Rex walked slowly toward the exit.

❉

Rex wandered down the empty corridor. Unlike on the base, the hallways were dark. He took a left, found the staircase, and quickly made his way up. His knee was no longer a hindrance; it was completely healed. He was anxious to check out the station and find Mei.

He could already tell that the station was much different than the Moon-X base. Exposed titanium piping lined the aluminum walls and ceilings. The station looked less livable and less refined. He did not have time to form any expectations about what the Russian space station would look like, but he imagined it would have resembled the Moon-X facility since the Russians helped to build the base. This, however, was not the case.

As Rex made his way up the stairs he wondered what Hendricks would say when Ed told him that he had quit and gotten on the shuttle, albeit inadvertently. Ed would not know that Rex had intended to return to the base unless Feng Feng had told him. He hoped that Feng Feng told Ed the whole story, but Rex knew that Ed might still not believe that Rex did not intentionally get on the shuttle, especially after their confrontation in the hangar.

When he reached the second floor, Rex was taken aback by what he saw. There was a large open space with an expansive window displaying a clear view of the illuminated earth against the backdrop of outer space. Rex realized that the station orbited the planet, and he was now much closer to it than he had been in a long while. Rex also noted that the earth was enormous in comparison to the moon, which he could now admire from afar.

For the first time, Rex experienced a tinge of nostalgia for home. He missed the colors of Earth and the light. Seeing the earth this close evoked a visceral response. Then he noticed the people around him. There were a few Russian crewmembers walking around, including several people from the base, but no military personnel were present. Rex made his way to the edge of the room to take in the panoramic view. After a few minutes, he turned his attention back to finding Mei. He looked around for someone in the crowd who might have information. He spied Xiao sitting on the floor a few meters away. Rex walked over to him and sat down. Xiao was eating some round gummy candies. Xiao held out his sweaty palm to offer Rex some candy, which he refused. Rex rested a moment.

Xiao finished chewing one candy, popped another one into his mouth, and then started talking and chewing at the same time. "Had a little run-in with the soldiers, eh?"

"You heard?"

"Yeah," Xiao said, "what were you doing?"

"That wasn't supposed to happen. I was trying to help Mei get home. Have you seen her?"

"I saw her go with that big Russian scientist friend of yours," Xiao said. "I haven't seen her since."

"You mean Sergei?"

"Yes."

This was all the information that Rex needed from Xiao, but he felt it would be rude to get up and walk away abruptly, so he continued asking him for other useful information. "Do you know when they are taking us back to Earth?"

"We're stuck," Xiao said. "The shuttle is broken. We don't know when it will be fixed, and we haven't heard if anyone is sending another shuttle up here to get us."

"Where are we all staying?"

"Here, as you can see. They have a few extra sleep pods on the fifth floor, but not enough for everyone."

"So we're on our own up here?"

"Pretty much," Xiao said.

"What about the Russian military, are they hostile?"

"They're keeping to themselves for the most part. You'll see a few around, especially in the cafeteria, but they seem too preoccupied to mind us much."

"Where is the cafeteria?"

"Fourth floor."

"And the control room?"

"Third floor, along with the labs."

"Facilities?"

"Showers are only on the fifth floor; there's a privy at the end of the hall on every floor except the sixth."

"Why? What's up there?"

"Storage and docking."

"What about communications? Any contact with friends on the ground?"

"They're up, but we are blocked—sort of."

Rex perked up. "Sort of?"

"Yes, two of us figured out how to circumvent the Russian security blocks."

"Excellent," Rex said. "And I assume you are one of the two?"

Xiao nodded.

"And who's the other?"

Xiao looked up and tilted his head to his right toward Li Ling, who was leaning against the wall, talking to two shorter men.

"Good to know. Can you send a message for me?"

"Yes, but not now. I don't want to draw attention to myself and start sending messages for everyone here."

"Got it. Thank you." Rex felt this was a good time to make his exit.

As he stood up, Xiao touched his arm to get his attention. "Stay away from the third floor."

"Why, other than the obvious?"

"I heard some of the soldiers talking in the cafeteria; they are supposed to leave us alone, unless we get in their way."

"And going to the third floor is getting in their way?"

"Yes."

"Thanks."

Rex walked back to the stairwell and ascended to the fifth floor to find Mei. The stairwell was made entirely of thin aluminum that clanged and banged as he climbed the stairs. The space station was built five years before the moon base, but it looked as if it were twenty years older. The lounge was inviting but only because of the large window and bright lighting. Rex considered taking a peek at the third floor, but he decided to save that for later. Now, he needed to find Mei. He did not know how to approach her after tricking her into leaving the base. He hoped, however, she would understand that he and Feng Feng had her best interests in mind, no matter how abominably their plan had unfolded.

Rex reached the fifth floor. All of the doors to the crew's quarters were closed. He slowly walked down the dark, narrow corridor. He put his ear against each door as he passed, hoping to hear a familiar voice. He was halfway down the hall when he heard Sergei's voice. Rex knocked on the door. Sergei answered and Mei was with him. She was sitting cross-legged on the floor. Sergei smiled and welcomed Rex with a bear hug. Sergei looked even more disheveled than he had while on the base. His beard was fuller and his hair looked unwashed. His gray uniform only highlighted the pallor of Sergei's skin.

"Good to see you, Rexi." Sergei stepped back, allowing Rex to enter the small room. Sergei's quarters were about half of the size of the rooms on the base. It was also dark gray with similarly colored furniture. There was a small cot against the wall, a tall closet to the side, and nothing else. Rex could not imagine that Sergei fit in his bed.

Sergei put his hand on Rex's shoulder. "It's too bad that Feng Feng did not get on the shuttle too. I've been explaining to Mei how bad things have gotten up here."

Rex looked over at Mei. She was staring at him in such a way that Rex could not tell whether she was angry or extremely pensive. He sat on the floor beside her.

"I'm sorry," Rex said as he reached out to hug her.

Mei did not move away, and (to his great relief) she returned the gesture. Then, very abruptly, she pushed him away. "I'm very displeased with you, Rex."

"I was trying to help."

"It's not your place to make decisions for me."

Sergei interrupted, "Rexi, it's really good to see you, but I have to go do some work, and you guys have some catching up to do. You can both stay here as long as you want. I'll come find you in about an hour." Rex nodded to indicate that he had heard Sergei. Mei continued looking down at the floor.

After Sergei had left, Rex placed his hand on Mei's arm. "I know. It wasn't right, and it wasn't supposed to happen like that."

"Like what? You getting trapped on the shuttle?"

"That's not what I mean."

"What do you mean?"

"Never in a million years did I think anyone would get hurt, let alone Wes," Rex said.

"What?"

"Didn't you see?"

"See what?"

"Wes tried to help me, and they killed him."

Mei covered half of her face with her hand. "I only saw you fighting with the Russians in the airlock, and then I knew you never meant to go with me."

"I was only trying to help."

"And Wes was trying to help, too?"

"Yes, he stepped in when he saw me being attacked, but he didn't know what we were doing."

"Of course, another dupe."

"I feel bad enough already, Mei."

Mei pushed his hand off of her arm and stood up and sat back down on Sergei's bed, leaving Rex alone on the floor.

"I wanted you to be safe. I wasn't thinking about anything else. I was stupid."

Mei nodded. "Yes, you were stupid."

"I know."

"And Feng Feng?"

"He and Dana made it back to the base." Rex scooted himself closer to the bed. "We had to do it, Mei. We knew you'd never leave the base willingly."

Mei slapped her chest as she spoke. "That's my choice."

"Just think about that for a moment. What would you have done if it were Dana?"

"I don't care about Dana," Mei said.

"You don't mean that."

"Yes, I do. I don't know her and her private business is her own. She can take care of herself."

"Your situation is special, Mei. You have to admit that."

"I don't have to do anything."

"Of course," Rex said. "I just didn't want to see anything bad happen to you."

"So ship me off?"

"I knew you might never forgive me, but I care about you, Mei. I only wanted to protect you. I put a note in my bag, hoping you'd find it and understand."

"Yes, I saw that I had your bag. Another trick!" Mei stood up and reached behind Sergei's bed and pulled out Rex's bag and pushed it over to him with her foot. "Show me. Show me your note."

Rex pulled out one of the moon rocks he had left for her and tossed it to her. Mei caught it in her right hand. She sat down on the bed and examined it.

"I thought you might want to take a piece with you," Rex said. Then he pulled out the paper he had torn from the anthology and passed it to Mei. "Here."

Mei put down the rock and accepted the paper. She read it silently. When she was finished, she crumpled the paper and threw it at Rex. "You're an idiot, Rex, a *big* idiot. Don't talk to me." Mei lay down flat on the bed and turned her body away from him.

Rex stood up from the floor and sat down on the bed next to Mei.

"I know," he said.

He gave her another hug and then they both reclined in unison. They rested there together in silence with their eyes closed, waiting for Sergei to return.

CHAPTER TWENTY

R EX FELT SOMEONE tugging at his sleeve. He opened his eyes
and saw Sergei standing next to him. Sergei motioned for him to
get up and follow him. "Come, Rexi, we have much to discuss."
Rex sat up. Mei was still sound asleep. He got up and followed Sergei into
the hall.

They descended the staircase to the third floor. Before allowing Rex
to enter the third-floor hallway, Sergei checked to see if anyone else was
around. He hesitated for a moment and then signaled for Rex to follow
him. Rex stepped out and walked behind Sergei as quickly as he could.
They passed the control room without anyone noticing and walked into
Sergei's lab. Sergei shut the door and turned on half of the lights, which
were bright enough to light up the entire room. The lab was about the
same size as the medical bay, but there was a large table in the middle
of the room with four chairs, and it was full of drop down translucent
computer screens and spare electrical parts for the station instead of medical equipment.

"What's going on?" Rex asked. "What was that message about that
ship that you sent to Pops?"

Sergei sat down at the table. "I'll get to that in a minute."

Rex sat down adjacent to him. "All right." He sat back in his seat.

"I think I found out what happened to the *Minerva*."

Hearing Sergei speak those words stopped all of the other thoughts
swimming around Rex's mind. The *Minerva* was the furthest subject from
his mind since he had arrived on the station. He was consumed with

worry about his mere presence on the Russian station, what Hendricks thought about his departure, the unfortunate fate of Wes, and Mei in general. Now, the mention of the *Minerva* interrupted all of these concerns.

"What?"

"I found something I overlooked before."

Rex leaned in toward Sergei. "What did you find?"

"Before I get into it, tell me: did you find out anything in the lab?"

"Nothing definitive. I was working on a theory that they encountered some space turbulence."

"And what became of that theory?"

"I can't prove it."

"Well," Sergei said, "I think I found out what happened, but you have to keep this to yourself, though."

"Everything?"

"Yes, and you have to swear."

"Of course, but can I tell Mei your theory about the *Minerva*? She wants to know what happened to Quon."

Sergei thought for a moment. "Okay."

"Tell me. What did you find?"

Sergei placed both of his fists on the table. "I found extra wiring around the ship."

"So?"

"There was extra wiring within vital points around the ship that served no known function."

"Didn't you look at the ship when it was completed?"

"Yes, but I was using my own checklist. I would not have been looking for extra components, only missing ones."

"What do you think the wiring was for?"

"Someone targeted the most vulnerable parts of the ship and placed wiring around them. What does that sound like to you?"

"Sabotage."

"Someone could remotely send a signal, causing a fire or explosion."

"Are you sure?"

Sergei stood up and pulled down a computer screen. He opened a diagram of the ship. Rex stood next to Sergei, who pointed to various areas of the ship. "Here, this is the engine." He moved his hand to the left. "This is the flight deck." He slid his hand to the right. "Here are the steering thrusters, and here's the ventilation system, and there is no reason for stray wires in any of those places."

"Is there any other explanation?"

"I designed the ship. I did not authorize these changes. This was done deliberately behind my back."

"Maybe someone wanted to control the ship."

"Or destroy it," Sergei said.

"Have you told anyone else about this?"

"There's no one left to talk to," Sergei said.

"What do you mean?"

"I can't locate the other two engineers I worked with. Every time I ask someone where they are, they give me a new location. When I inquire there, they tell me they've been reassigned to another place, and that only means one thing."

"What?"

"They've been *disappeared*."

"Can that really happen?"

Sergei laughed. "Ever hear of Siberia?"

Rex nodded. "Is there anyone else you can talk to about this?"

"No, and I don't think I should."

"What would be the motive for destroying the ship?"

"They never meant for the *Minerva* to reach Mars."

"But why?"

"A trillion reasons," Sergei said.

"But how can you know for sure?"

"I have a feeling."

"Do you have any other proof?"

"Of the wiring, yes, of motives, no."

"There might be some other explanation."

"Not for me," Sergei said.

"Maybe the design plan you found was someone's rough draft," Rex said, "or maybe the wires were installed for control or sabotage, but the space turbulence set off the mechanism by accident. Then we would both be partly right."

"I'm sure the military did it, and I think they were hoping that it would cause the collaboration on the base to fall apart especially if Russian funds were taken away from Moon-X."

"But it didn't stop Moon-X from carrying on."

"No," Sergei said, "and then we got kicked off the base for no reason."

"Right."

"Now they have an excuse to take over the whole base."

"You think they set this up?"

"It worked out well for a country who doesn't want nuclear fusion," Sergei said.

"Then why invest in Moon-X to begin with?"

"How does one explain to the populous that international collaboration for a moon base is bad for the country?"

"I'm sure they could come up with some excuse."

"You're thinking like a scientist, Rex. You must try to think like a politician."

"Let's see what Pops thinks."

"You were able to bring him?"

"Yes, luckily I had him on when I was forced aboard."

"I can't plug him in to the main system," Sergei said.

"Why not?"

"Are you kidding, Rex? If anyone found out that I helped an American snoop around the station's military computers, they'd shoot me."

"Is there any way that we can work with Pops?"

"We can try my computer," Sergei said, "but I have to disable any connectivity into the rest of the station."

"Of course."

Sergei punched a few controls on the table. A holographic keyboard appeared and a gel pad slid out from the side of the table. Rex removed the nanodot from behind his ear and submerged it into the gel pad. There was not enough capacity in Sergei's computer for Pops's image to manifest, so they waited for him to speak up. There were no security restrictions on Pops in Sergei's computer so they could both hear him.

"Where the heck am I?" Pops asked.

"Pops, we're on the Russian space station and—"

Pops interrupted. "Space station! What in tarnation are we doing on the space station?"

"Pops, I'll explain later."

"Does this have to do with that scuffle you got us into back on the moon?"

"Yes, but let's talk about that later. Right now, I need your help with something."

"I'll bet," Pops said. "This is some pickle you've gotten us into. Are you finally taking me home?"

"Yes."

"Well, thank goodness for that. When do we get home?"

"I don't know," Rex said.

"You don't know? How long are we going to be up here, then?"

"I don't know."

"You better get us out of here."

"Yes, Pops, but right now I need you to do some work. You have access to Sergei's computer, and we want you to review some data and give us your assessment."

"This doesn't feel right," Pops said.

"How so?"

"I don't know if I can work under these conditions."

"You're fine, Pops."

"I'm confined to a personal computer on the Russian space station. I'm not fine."

"Just look at the data it's important."

"I feel claustrophobic."

Sergei threw up his arms. "What is going on here?"

Rex tried to keep Sergei calm. "Just give me a minute to help Pops understand."

Pops continued complaining. "No, it's not okay; the walls are closing in on me."

"There are no walls," Rex said. "Nothing is closing in on you. Just look at the data."

"What am I supposed to be looking for?"

"There's a diagram of the *Minerva* that Sergei found that shows some extra wiring that he did not authorize. I want to you take a look at that diagram, analyze it, put into context with all of your other data about the *Minerva*, and tell us if you think the wiring was used for sabotage."

"Let me see." Rex and Sergei remained silent while they waited for Pops to do his analysis. "There are a few suspicious messages here."

"What do they say?" Rex asked.

"They say, 'Get Pops out of this box and set him free.'"

"Pops, be serious."

"All right, there's no information about the wiring. Nothing confirms sabotage."

"You can't find any information about the wiring at all?" Rex asked.

"Nope," Pops said. "You're welcome."

"Thank you," Rex said.

Sergei removed the nanodot from the gel pad and handed it back to Rex. "I still stand by my sabotage theory."

Rex put the nanodot back behind his ear. "Can you keep searching through your network for more information?"

"I'm trying," Sergei said, "but now that the military has taken over the station, I'm stuck."

"Why didn't they send you home with Nik and Yelena?" Rex asked.

"They need me to help with space station repairs. The commander doesn't understand how the station works, and the military is mostly trained in flight, weapons, or communications—not engineering."

"I see."

"You're lucky you got off the base, you know."

"I didn't mean to, and I shouldn't be here."

"All the same," Sergei said, "you are better off here."

"Why do you say that?"

"You know that big ship they have parked outside the base?"

"Yes, what is it?"

"They had all the military scientists working on it, and that means that it is carrying a weapon. I'm guessing it's a type of energy weapon, and they're ready to test it."

"Why put it on a ship and not the space station?"

"I don't know," Sergei said. "Maybe they don't want to be accused of weaponizing the space station."

"Ironic."

"It's scary. The military has no accountability up here—none."

"Sergei, why are you telling me all of this?"

"I don't like what's happening, and I can't talk to anyone up here about it."

"I know how you feel."

"I know. That's why I can talk to you. I spent twelve years building that ship. I left my wife and daughter for a year to work up here, thinking I was accomplishing something. They destroyed it all, and for what? I at least deserve to know the truth about what happened, and so do you."

"What can you do now?"

"There's nothing I can do," Sergei said. "I just want to go home."

"I get it."

"You better go check on Mei," Sergei said.

"Right," Rex said as he exited the room.

CHAPTER TWENTY-ONE

REX SAT WITH Mei near the back of the cafeteria to stay away from the Russian soldiers. He attempted to eat his potatoes but found that the food quality on the space station was even worse than on the base. The freeze-dried food did not bother him as much as the metallic-tasting water they used to reconstitute it. Mei set her fork down on the table in disgust. They both stopped pretending to eat.

"You know, I quit the company," he said. "I don't know what's going to happen when I get home."

"Why would you do that?" Mei kicked Rex under the table.

"I had a fight with Ed and quit."

"What will you do now?"

"I don't know. All my work was for nothing. They are going to continue with the fusion project, but they will use deuterium and create radioactive waste. That's exactly what I wanted to avoid. That was my whole reason for working on the base, besides being closer to Avery."

"Maybe things will calm down and the mining will continue," Mei said.

"It can't. The Russians are burning all of the helium-3. It's over."

"Maybe there's another material?"

"No, it will take years of research."

"Your country is different. You can find another project. I'm going to have to work extra hard to keep my position when I get back."

"I'm sorry, Mei. I feel bad. I really do, and I blame myself for Wes."

"It was those soldiers," Mei said. "You couldn't have known they'd react like they did."

"I caused the situation."

"I don't approve of you tricking me, but what they did to Wes was murder." Before Rex could respond, the tall Russian soldier that he had fought with while trying to leave the shuttle entered the room and sat down with his friends at another table. "Speak of your devil," she said.

Rex stared at the soldier as he sat talking with another fellow soldier. Rex continued to glare at them as they got up from their table to get food from the counter. Rex fidgeted in his seat. He was incensed by the soldier's presence. Mei stretched her arm out across the table and took Rex's hand. "There's nothing we can do now."

"We shouldn't be here," Rex said. "I was wrong to put you on that shuttle."

Mei stood up and walked around to Rex's side of the table. "Come on, let's go to the lounge."

As Rex rose, the base commander marched confidently into the cafeteria accompanied by a soldier twice the size of the one Rex had fought with earlier. The commander looked at Rex and quickly walked over to him and Mei, blocking their egress. He shook hands with Rex and then Mei. "I'm Commander Usov. Welcome aboard. Mr. Kanin, would you mind coming with me?"

Rex understood there was no choice in the request. "Of course."

"Excuse us, Mrs. Wan." The commander and Rex turned to leave.

Rex followed the commander and the large soldier out of the cafeteria, down the hall, and into a small office by the control room. The soldier stood in the doorway while Rex and the commander went inside. Rex gathered that this was the commander's office. There was a large desk with a touchscreen computer built in, one chair in front of the desk, one behind it, and a tiny window opening up to the stars on the wall behind the desk.

The commander motioned for Rex to sit down, and he complied. Then the commander sat behind his desk and smiled. This was unnerving to Rex since he had expected the commander to exude more hostility toward him.

"I hear you were resistant to board the shuttle," the commander said.

"Yes," Rex said. "I did not mean to board the ship."

"How did it happen that you arrived at my shuttle's door then?"

"I was helping a friend."

"Mrs. Wan?"

"Yes," Rex said.

"Well, no matter." The commander said. "We are happy to have you."

"Can I go back?"

The commander shook his head. "The shuttle is under repair."

"So I've heard," Rex said. "Can I leave when it's fixed?"

"You are fortunate to be here."

"Fortunate? Your soldiers forced me onto the shuttle and killed a man."

"You are fortunate that it was not you."

"They didn't have to kill him."

"It was an accident. I understand that he was trying to help you, correct?"

"Yes, your men were attacking me."

The commander laughed. "My men were helping you aboard."

"Is that what you call it?" Rex

"In any event, you are better off here. Things may get even more unpleasant on the base, especially if we are not allowed entry."

"They'll never let you in," Rex said.

"Then they will suffer the consequences."

"But they are unarmed."

The commander smirked. "If the company refuses to let us in, and we take the base, we are simply reappropriating our property. We invested in Moon-X."

"And you stopped funding Moon-X."

"Why don't you ask your boss where our investment money is, then?"

"Is that what this is about?"

"No. We were talking about you. Maybe you should start considering your own position."

"Is that a threat?"

"Not at all. If there was some reason for us not to enter the base that you knew of, perhaps you could stop some of this."

"I don't know what you are talking about."

"If there were dangerous weapons on the base, we might think twice about going in."

"I just told you," Rex said, "they are unarmed."

"Are they?" The commander watched Rex's reaction closely.

Rex was careful not to show any concern, even though his stomach was cramping up. "You know I'm only doing research in the fusion lab, using non-radioactive materials."

"Perhaps, but that doesn't mean that the Americans aren't hiding other weapons."

"I wouldn't know."

"What does the company think about you abandoning your post?"

"I didn't abandon my post, I was kidnapped."

"Did you tell them that?" the commander asked.

"You know I can't communicate with them."

"Yes, so what do you think the company is thinking?"

"I don't know."

"What do you think your government is thinking?"

Rex glared at the commander.

The commander leaned forward in his chair. "I'll tell you what they are thinking. They are thinking you are a traitor."

Rex shook his head. "No, I will explain everything."

"If you get the chance."

"Another threat?"

"I'm only saying that I know you don't have a job to return to, and that your own country will imprison you, and that my country happens to need a physicist like yourself."

"You're offering me a job?" Rex wondered how the commander could know that he had quit. He reasoned that the commander was either merely hypothesizing or that the commander had intercepted a communication between Ed and Hendricks.

"Yes."

"And if I refuse?"

"There are some Russian officers on the ground who may be more persuasive."

"So many threats."

"Just offering you the opportunity to stop any more unfortunate incidents," the commander said, "and a job."

Rex stood up. "I'm leaving now."

"Of course, and if you decide that you have some information to share, my door is always open."

Rex turned and left without responding. He was relieved that the commander did not use any physical force on him, but he was a little scared that he still might. He wanted to get away from the commander's office as quickly as he could. The large soldier was still standing outside the door, but he did not impede Rex's egress.

❄

Rex entered the lounge. Everyone looked even more uncomfortable than they had when Rex was there earlier. Several people were reading, while others had congregated to talk, and some paced back and forth by the window. Mei and Sergei sat on the floor near the large window. The moon was full and bright and Rex admired it for a moment. He turned around and spied Mei. Sergei motioned for him to sit down. "We've been waiting for you, Rexi." Rex took a seat adjacent to Mei.

"We're going to play three-player mahjong," Mei said. She removed the north wind tile, the bamboo tiles numbered two through eight, and then the four season tiles. Then she scrambled the remaining blocks. She pushed some tiles over to Rex. "Here, build your wall."

"Where did you get this set?"

"I borrowed it from Junjie," Mei said. Rex and Sergei each chose thirteen tiles while Mei picked up fourteen. They were ready to start to the game.

"This is like on the base, except we're missing the baijiu," Mei said. "I could use some right now, actually."

"I've got some vodka if you like," Sergei said, taking out a small flask from his back pocket. Mei politely refused. Sergei took a quick sip and then offered some to Rex. He also refused—not that he did not want it, but he declined for Mei's sake. Mei started the game; she discarded a three-dot tile.

Rex picked up the tile. "Chow!" He placed three sequential dot tiles, numbered one through three, and discarded an east wind tile. He thought that playing mahjong in the space station lounge, as strange as the circumstances were, was comforting.

"You're off to a strong start," Mei said.

Sergei played his hand. "What did the commander want?"

"He offered me a job," Rex said.

Mei looked up at Rex. "He's not serious?" Mei picked up a tile and quickly discarded it.

"Oh, yes. He said mother Russia needed more physicists, and my government would put me in jail when I got home."

"Did he threaten you?"

Rex nodded. "You could say that. And he wanted me to disclose all of my nuclear secrets."

"You don't have any secrets, do you, Rexi?" Sergei pushed Rex's arm jokingly.

"You know what they say," Rex said, "'to whom you confide your secrets, you resign your liberty.'"

"Yes," Sergei said, "and three can keep a secret if two of them are dead."

"Talk doesn't cook rice. Rex, it's your turn."

"Right." Rex picked up a tile and discarded a six-dot.

Mei grabbed it. "Pong!" She set down three six-dot tiles.

Rex turned to Sergei. "What do you think will happen when we get back to Earth?"

"When we get back, I'm going home. Mei's going home. You might be stuck."

"They can't keep me a prisoner forever."

"That's why they'll say you defected," Sergei said.

"But I'm not going to."

Sergei picked up a tile. "Who's going to know?"

Mei focused on Rex. "You have to get a message to the company."

"I agree," Sergei said.

"Sergei, can you help him?"

"He doesn't have to," Rex said. "I can find a way to get through."

Sergei raised an eyebrow. "Really?"

"Yes," Rex said. "In fact, I should probably go do it after this game before anything else happens."

The rest of the game went very quickly. Mei set down three more sets and declared mahjong after revealing her pair of green dragons, completing her hand. Before starting another round, Rex excused himself to go talk to Xiao. They agreed to resume the game when he returned.

❋

Xiao was sleeping propped up against the back wall of the room behind Yun and Junjie, who were talking about the broken shuttle. Rex hesitated before waking Xiao, but did so anyway. He put his hand on his shoulder and lightly jostled him. Xiao stirred but did not wake. Rex nudged Xiao a little harder. He woke up, startled.

"Xiao, can you help me get through to the company now?"

"Maybe," Xiao said without getting up.

Rex sat down next to him. "Does that mean that communications are working?"

"Yes."

"Can you get me through to the Moon-X HQ?"

"Yes, but it's risky."

"I know," Rex said, "and I really appreciate your help."

"How much do you appreciate my help?"

Rex understood that Xiao was looking for something. "What can I do for you?"

Xiao sat up. "I don't know. What do you have?"

"Not much. I didn't expect to be here."

"What about your Russian friend over there?"

Rex thought for a moment. "Wait here." He walked back over to Sergei and asked him for his flask. Sergei was reluctant to give it to him but did so. Rex took the flask back to Xiao and presented it to him surreptitiously.

Xiao took it. "Okay, who do you want to contact?"

"Ty in the Nevada facility."

Xiao took out his scroll computer from under his blanket and unrolled it, being careful to keep it partially covered. He worked on making contact. Rex sat back and relaxed, waiting for Xiao to make the connection. Xiao continued working intensely. He motioned for Rex to come closer and hunch down. Xiao spread the blanket over Rex's lap and transferred the graphene scroll over to him.

"You have three minutes," Xiao said. "Speak softly and don't let anyone see."

Rex nodded, even though he was sure everyone in the room knew what they were up to. Xiao stood and stretched to give him some cover. Rex lay down and turned to face the wall with his back to the rest of the room. He heard Ty answer but he could not see him on the screen.

"Ty?" Rex asked.

"Yes. Rex, is that you?"

"It's me. I'm on the Russian space station."

"I heard. What happened?"

"It was an accident. I was helping Mei get aboard and then they grabbed me."

"Why did you have to help Mei?"

"I'll explain later."

"You know, Hendricks is fuming. He doesn't know what to think. He says you quit."

"Yes, I did, but I didn't mean to get on the shuttle. I tried to run away, but the Russian soldiers nabbed me."

"Is there any way to get back to the base?"

"No, and I keep hearing how dangerous it is to be there. Their ship is carrying a secret weapon; you have to let Hendricks know."

"I'll find him right away," Ty said.

"Can you tell Hendricks that I didn't mean to get on that shuttle?"

"Yes, of course. How are they treating you?"

"Okay for now—not sure how it will go once I get on the ground."

"You know, Rex, the company can't help you in Russia."

"I understand, but whatever they say, I'm not defecting."

"It's going to be hard to explain this to Hendricks. He's going berserk. He's been meeting with the military. The major is already saying that you switched sides."

"Ty, I've never been on a side. I haven't done anything wrong, except try to help a friend."

"That may be, but you need to get here to defend yourself."

"I would if I could, you know that."

"Yes," Ty said, "I believe you."

"Will you talk to Hendricks?"

"Yes."

"Look, I'm running out of time. I think the base is in danger. If the Russians go in, it could be bad."

"Of course it would be bad," Ty said.

"No, I mean there are things the military is hiding. It could be really bad."

Ty was silent.

"Ty, are you there?"

"Yes, don't say any more, Rex. We don't know who could be listening, and you're already in enough hot water."

"Understood, but will you talk to Hendricks?"

"Yes." Xiao tapped Rex with his foot to warn him to end the call. "Ty, I have to go." The connection was cut off. Xiao sat back down and took the scroll. He rolled it up and placed it under his bag.

"Thanks, Xiao."

"Sounds like someone's in trouble," Xiao said.

"Yeah. It'll be all right. I just have to get home."

"How are you going to manage that?"

Rex shook his head. "I don't know."

As Rex and Xiao were talking, five soldiers descended the staircase and started scouring the lounge, looking for something. Xiao nudged Rex and whispered, "They're looking for communication devices."

"Do you think they detected my call?"

"Yes," Xiao said.

"What do we do?"

"Nothing. Just watch them."

Rex took Xiao's advice. He watched the soldiers move around the room, checking to see if they could find anyone using any devices. A young gangly soldier stopped by Li Ling and searched her bag. They did not find anything. He turned away and continued his search. Xiao looked nervous. The young soldier approached them.

"He's coming," Rex said.

Xiao pushed his scroll behind Rex's back.

"What do you want me to do with it?"

"Hide it!"

Rex sat on the scroll. The soldier came up to Xiao and grabbed his blanket. Finding nothing, he threw it back down. He picked up Xiao's bag and dumped out its contents. Small bags of Asian candy and snack-mix fell to the ground. The soldier knelt and examined the packages. He picked up two bags of strawberry mochi candy and one bag of prawn crackers.

"I have to requisition these," the soldier said as he stood up.

"Why?" Xiao asked.

"Security," the soldier said.

"That's ridiculous!"

"If you have problem, take it up with Commander Usov," he said as he walked away.

Xiao's face flushed. He was clearly angry. He turned to Rex. "He should have paid me for that!"

"At least he didn't get the computer."

"Yeah, but strawberry is my favorite. I traded two blank x-drives to get those."

"Sorry," Rex said. "Maybe I should have waited longer to make that call."

"It's all right. I'm surprised they didn't search us sooner. I mean, it only took those oafs seven hours to figure that a room full of the world's top scientists might be able to hack through their rudimentary security systems."

"If I have the chance," Rex said, "I'll grab something from one of the soldiers for you."

Xiao smiled. "Thank you."

Rex waited for the soldiers to leave and then slid Xiao's computer back over to him. The room was abuzz with chatter about the hostility of the soldiers. Rex excused himself and returned to the mahjong game with Mei and Sergei. Mei won, as always. They played late into the evening. When it was time to retire, Sergei offered to share his room with Rex and Mei. Since the lounge was crowded, Rex and Mei accepted. They returned to Sergei's quarters where he gave them two blankets each. With such limited resources on the space station, Rex felt fortunate enough to be able to stay with Sergei and hide away from the soldiers for a few hours. The floor was as cold as the air. Mei rolled her body next to Rex's and he put his arm under her head. They held each other for heat as much as for comfort as they tried to fall asleep to the sound of Sergei's vibrant snore.

CHAPTER TWENTY-TWO

REX AND MEI spent most of their day in the lounge. He preferred to spend his time in the company of his old colleagues rather than trying to dodge the Russian soldiers around the rest of the station. The general mood in the lounge was tense. The lack of information about when they would be leaving made everyone antsy—not to mention the fact that the deadline for permitting a Russian inspection of the base had already passed. Everyone waited for some news about whether the Russians were going to make good on their threat to enter the base by force.

Rex and Mei sat in front of the window, not saying much to each other. The view of Earth from the lounge kept them entertained for a good while. They had an early dinner with Sergei and were now waiting for him to rejoin them after he was finished with his work. Suddenly, there were some rumblings amongst the group. Li Ling ran to the window and screamed and pointed frantically at the moon. Others rushed in behind her. Rex stood up and Mei followed. They pushed their way closer to the window before the crowd shoved them farther back to where they wouldn't be able to see as well. Rex saw Mei elbow a few people in defense of her position.

Rex looked out at the moon and saw a flash of red light, and then another. He heard a voice in the crowd asking what it was. Nobody had an answer. They watched together, looking for clues. There was a bright orange explosion, and the crowd gasped in unison. Rex's stomach flipped and sank. He was sure that it was the hidden nuclear weapons exploding but hoped that it was not so.

"They hit the base," someone said.

"Maybe it's the Americans going after those ships."

"No, they blew up the base!"

"They attacked the base!" Sergei shouted from the back of the crowd. This comment silenced them all.

There were three more flashes of orange light. The moon shined bright as a newborn star. Rex squinted his eyes and looked away. When he looked back, the moon had been transformed from a luminescent floating pearl into a ruby-colored orb. The angry red surface expanded and contracted like an eruptive variable star. Rex could hardly believe his eyes. He was transfixed and could not look away. Mei gasped and grabbed his arm.

Sergei made his way through the crowd until he reached Rex and Mei. "The moon is on fire!"

"This isn't possible!" someone shouted.

"I don't like this," said another.

Just when the moon seemed to be stabilizing, it shrank. Its edges became noticeably less round and more oblong. The top of the misshapen sphere inverted and slowly dissolved into itself. As it did so, several red flames shot out from its surface like giant solar flares. The flares merged, and for several minutes the moon resembled a pulsar. Finally, the moon exploded like a supernova, sending flaming debris hurling through space. The blanket of space smothered the light from the burning embers as they travelled farther apart. Then it was dark. There was no moon at all and the light of the moon was extinguished. The lounge became darker and the stars more dim.

Rex backed away from the window. Mei and Sergei followed him over to the beam in the middle of the room.

"Did that really happen?" Rex asked.

"I don't even know what that was," Sergei said.

Rex noticed that Mei's hands were shaking as she combed her fingers through her hair several times in a row. "They blew up the moon," Mei whispered.

Rex turned to Sergei. "Did they mean to do it?"

"I don't know. I can't imagine why anyone would intentionally do that."

"Maybe it was the Americans," Mei said.

Rex did not want to believe it. Then he thought about the nukes. "If they did, it was an accident."

"Hell of an accident," Sergei said.

Rex stepped closer to Sergei and spoke in a low voice, "Could it have been that new weapon?"

"What weapon?" Mei asked.

Sergei gave Rex an admonishing look. Then he addressed Mei. "The ship they sent had a directed energy weapon on it. Something experimental."

Mei looked back at Rex. "Why didn't you tell me?"

"It wasn't something I could speak freely about."

"I warned Rex about it in confidence," Sergei said.

"What kind of weapon can do that?" Mei asked.

"No weapon alone can do that," Sergei said. "There must be more to this than we know."

Before they could explore the topic further, loud clanging sounds came from the station's outer hull like hail hitting the metal roof of a car. Moon rock debris was pummeling the station.

Rex turned to Sergei. "Can the station withstand these strikes?"

"The Kevlar shielding will hold for a while," Sergei said, "but I don't know for how long."

A few of the crewmembers by the window shrieked. Everyone in the lounge instinctively backed away from the window, even though there was no place to go for refuge.

"Is the window secure?" Mei asked Sergei.

"Just as sturdy as the rest of the station, maybe even more so. It's made of fused silica with a nanocellulose coating."

"I wish I had a nanocellulose coating," Mei said.

"We'll get through this," Sergei said.

"What do we do now?" Rex asked.

Sergei looked out the window. "We wait."

There was a loud crash and the station swayed. A few crewmembers fell to the deck. Rex struggled to remain standing. He held on to the beam, and Mei held on to Rex. Sergei was able to maintain his balance. People sat down. There was a loud pop and the lights went out. The emergency blue lights immediately came on, casting a spooky hue around everything and everyone in the lounge.

The aluminum walls of the station rumbled like thunder, as the outer steel hull suffered more impacts. A handful of titanium bolts fell from the ceiling along with three metal panels, hitting the crewmembers below. A bolt narrowly missed Rex's head. He put his arms up to shield himself. Sergei and Mei did the same. A few crewmembers screamed as they were struck by falling metal. Most people ran to the walls where nothing could fall on them. The beam that Rex leaned on for support slowly buckled. He heard the crunching sound of metal above him and looked up. Rex took Mei by the hand and motioned for Sergei to follow him. He led them to a vacant space under the stairwell to hunker down. As they sat down, the beam fell down on a table and crushed it.

Mei flung herself onto Rex. "The station's falling apart!"

Rex looked to Sergei for an answer. "It'll hold," Sergei said.

"Are you sure?"

"No, but the station's design is strong," Sergei said.

"I don't even want to say what I'm thinking," Mei said.

A giant rock flew by the window. Rex automatically ducked as a reflex. "Did you see that?"

"Yes," Sergei said.

"Can the station withstand a hit from something that size?" Rex asked. Sergei hesitated to respond. "Well?" Rex and Mei looked at Sergei, intensely awaiting his response.

"Maybe, but not multiple strikes from projectiles that size."

Mei let go of Rex and sat down farther away from him. She closed her eyes.

"Where are you going?" he asked.

"If I'm going to meet Quon, I don't want to do it while in another man's arms."

Before Rex could respond, the base stopped swaying and began vibrating strongly. A loud metallic creaking sound echoed through the lounge. He slid closer to Mei.

"They're moving the station," Sergei said.

Mei looked up at Sergei. "Is that good?"

"Yes, I think so," Sergei said. "They need to get us out of the debris field."

Rex was not so sure. "Can the station make it out of the debris field?"

"Yes. This tin can might not seem like much, but I can tell you it has good bones, as long as it can navigate around the big ones."

"Glad to hear it," Rex said.

Sergei half-smiled. "Good engineering."

The station stopped swaying and began to yaw. It was dizzying and Rex had to lie down.

Mei crouched down and placed her head on Rex's stomach. "What's going on?"

"We lost a stabilizer," Sergei said.

"Is that bad?" Mei asked.

"Depends," Sergei said.

Mei sat back up. "Depends on what?"

"Whether the commander or any of his men knows how to steer under these conditions."

Rex held on to Mei more tightly. She did not push him away. The station lurched and tilted to one side.

"Okay, that's bad," Sergei said.

Mei's face blanched. "Are we going to die?"

Sergei put his hand on her arm. "It's going to be a rough night." He stood up. "I'm going to the control room to offer my help."

"Do you know how to steer this thing?" Rex asked.

"In theory, yes," Sergei said.

Mei waved him on. "Go—run—before they flip this thing over."

Sergei did not waste any time running up the stairs. Rex and Mei remained under the staircase. Mei's face was now buried in Rex's chest while he sat up looking out the window. He feared that the window would shatter. He saw large boulders fly by and a few smaller ones. He shut his eyes in anticipation of imminent depressurization.

"I'm sorry, Mei," Rex said.

"For what?"

"For everything—for tricking you, for taking you here, for getting Wes killed—"

Mei interrupted him. "Don't talk like that—not now."

"I just want you to know—"

"Tell me what it's going to be like when we get back to Earth," Mei said. The station heaved and Mei hugged Rex tighter.

"We're going to walk on solid ground, eat real food, and breathe fresh air," Rex said.

"I could use some fresh air," Mei said.

"Me too," Rex said.

"Do you think Quon and Avery went like this?" Mei asked.

"I thought we weren't supposed to talk like that," Rex said.

"I hope they weren't alone when it happened," Mei said.

"I don't think they had time to know what even happened," Rex said.

"Why do you say that?"

"Sergei thinks it was sabotage," Rex said.

"Sabotage? That's a new theory," Mei said. "What did you find out, Rex? Tell me. I want to know before I die."

"We're not going to die," Rex said.

"We might," Mei said.

"We're not."

"Tell me."

"Sergei found some extra wiring around sensitive areas of the ship that he didn't put there."

"Who did?"

"He doesn't know."

"He thinks it was put there to sabotage the ship?"

"Yes," Rex said.

"Why would anyone do that?"

"I don't know. Maybe the Russian government never intended the mission to make it."

"Why?"

"Sergei thinks they wanted Moon-X to abandon the base," Rex said.

"If that's true, then we are in the lion's den," Mei said. She stretched out her legs. "Do you think it's true?"

"I don't know."

"I do," Mei said.

"Why's that?"

"Because there's no other explanation and I need to blame somebody," Mei said. "And they were definitely after the base." She sat up and looked out the window. "And the moon—what about the moon?"

"It's all gone," Rex said.

"Is this really happening?"

Rex wanted to tell Mei about the nukes but decided that was a secret he should keep. "If I had not seen it happen," Rex said, "I would not have believed it."

"I don't want to believe it," Mei said.

Rex nodded his head, even though he was dealing with his own disbelief. He was glad that they were together. The station continued to be bombarded by moon rocks for another forty-five minutes. He and Mei sat in silence for most of it, unlike some of the others who shrieked every time the space station suffered an impact.

After the impacts subsided, Rex hoped that the worst was over. He did not see any more pieces of debris floating by the window. Once it seemed that they were going to survive, people moved around the room again. Li Ling was even brave enough to go up to the window. It was dark but Rex could tell that it was her; she was the only woman with short hair. Li Ling pointed at the window. Xiao went over to her. She shouted loudly in Mandarin. Rex turned to Mei. "What did she say?"

"She said the debris is hitting the earth!"

Rex went to the window to take a look. He saw fiery lunar debris entering the earth's atmosphere. Some rocks were large, but many were small enough to be burned up by the atmosphere. He also saw that debris was getting caught in the earth's gravity, clumping together and circling the earth. He could only imagine the effect that the lunar shower was having on the earth below. It would be like a barrage of brimstone from above, and people likely had no time to prepare. Rex wanted to keep watching at the window, but the stress of the entire situation was fatiguing and he needed to rest. He returned to Mei and reclined on the floor under the stairs. Mei copied him. They watched out the window together in silence until their eyes couldn't stay open any longer.

CHAPTER TWENTY-THREE

REX WOKE UP alone under the stairs. The emergency lights were still on. He scanned the room for Mei but did not see her. At first he thought she might have gone to find some food or to use the restroom. He waited a good long while before getting up to see if she was nearby. Some people were sleeping on the floor, lining up their bodies with the walls of the room. A few people were up, talking softly. Rex noticed a woman pacing back and forth. It was dark, but as he moved closer he again recognized that it was Li Ling. He walked up to her and lightly touched her on the shoulder. "Are you okay?" Li Ling stopped pacing.

"I can't sleep," Li Ling said.

"I don't think anyone is really sleeping that well." Rex stood next to Li Ling, unsure of whether to put his arm around her as a comforting gesture.

"Do you think we're going to make it?" Li Ling asked.

"We seem to be out of danger," Rex said. "For now, at least."

"What did your Russian friend say?"

"He didn't have time to say much. He left to help the crew."

"Good."

"Did you see everything?"

"Unfortunately, yes," Li Ling said.

"Did you get through to anyone on the base before it happened?"

"Right before it started, I got through to Feng Feng."

Rex perked up and became fully attentive. "What did he say?"

"He wanted to know how you were. He said Ed scolded him greatly for leaving the base with you. Then we were cut off."

A cold chill came over Rex and he did not want to talk anymore. He imagined Feng Feng did not have any time to prepare or even figure out what was happening. Rex equivocated but decided that it was appropriate under the circumstances and hugged Li Ling.

Rex walked over to the window, which felt less threatening now that large boulders were no longer flying by. The space station was repositioned above the South Pole. Rex noted that the debris field was forming a ring around the earth's equator. The earth would now be experiencing adverse effects due to the loss of the moon. Most noticeably, the tides would be affected. The gravitational disruption would have cascading effects around the globe, such as earthquakes and volcanic eruptions. The floating debris would also destroy orbiting satellites in its way, disrupting communication and navigational systems. Rex understood that if they ever made it back to Earth, it would be a different world from the one they left. Mei grabbed Rex's arm. She looked especially pale, even in the blue light.

"Where'd you go?" Rex asked.

"I went to the loo," Mei said. "I tripped and fell on a loose wire and hurt my wrist."

"Why didn't you wake me?"

"I didn't want to disturb you."

"Are you all right?"

"No, I think it's sprained." Mei held up her left wrist for Rex to examine.

Rex ushered Mei out of the room. "Let's go find the doctor."

"How will we find him?"

They walked to the stairwell. "He's on the first level. He helped me when we first got here," Rex said as they descended the stairs.

"Do you think he's down there?"

"Let's see," Rex said.

The first level was darker than the lounge. There were only a few intermittently spaced emergency lights on the ceiling and a few did not work. Rex walked into the medical bay first and Mei followed closely behind him. Only one soft light emanated from the back of the room. They walked toward it. Rex saw the doctor kneeling on the floor, praying in his native language. He touched the doctor's shoulder. Dr. Gali looked up at Rex, clearly startled. "What's happening?"

"She needs your help," Rex said, motioning toward Mei.

Dr. Gali stood up but seemed unsteady. "Did we make it?"

"We are out of the way of the rocks and debris," Rex said.

"Thank goodness," Dr. Gali said.

Dr. Gali's hands trembled. Mei stepped forward and Rex once again made his request. "Dr. Gali, can you take a look at Mei?"

The doctor focused on Mei. "What's wrong, my dear?"

Mei held up her left wrist. "I fell and landed on it."

Dr. Gali sat Mei down on a cot and examined her hand. He pressed on her fingers. Then he rotated her wrist. Mei expressed her discomfort with a squeal. Without a word, the doctor went to get some supplies from the cupboard. He removed a clear bottle of liquid and another bottle of silver-colored powder.

"What's that?" Rex asked.

Dr. Gali took a syringe and needle from the drawer and walked back over to Mei. "It's an anti-inflammatory." The doctor unwrapped the syringe and affixed the needle.

"Like ibuprofen?" Mei asked.

Dr. Gali drew up some of the liquid and then transferred it into the bottle with the silver powder. He withdrew the needle and shook the bottle until all of the powder dissolved. "This is stronger. It binds to the inflamed tissue."

"How long does it last?"

"Forever." The doctor drew up half of the solution and then inserted the needle into Mei's left wrist and released the liquid.

"Really?"

"Yes, forever …unless you re-injure yourself." The doctor removed the needle.

"I'll be sure not to."

"Nothing to worry about," Dr. Gali said, "just a little sprain."

Mei looked at Dr. Gali. "Are you sure it's not broken?"

"Yes, I'm sure."

"There's something else,"

Dr. Gali looked up. "Yes?"

"I'm pregnant. Could my fall have hurt the baby?"

Dr. Gali raised one of his thick eyebrows. "Ah, now I understand why all the fuss to get you here."

"No, I'm not the father," Rex said.

"It's not my business." Dr. Gali turned to Mei. "Did you hit your stomach when you fell?"

"No, I landed on my wrist."

"Then I'm sure it's fine, dear. For now, just sit here and try to keep your wrist elevated. Now, if you two will excuse me, I'm going to go have a look around and see if anyone else needs my help." He took his leave and exited the room.

Rex pushed a cot closer to Mei. He rested his hand on her shoulder. She reached up, put her hand on top of his, and held it. Mei stroked a thick strand of her hair like she often did when she was worried. He tried to reassure her that all would be well; but, given all that had transpired, he was not so sure. They both reclined onto the cots. Rex tried to stay awake and keep Mei company, but he was exhausted and fell asleep.

Later that night, Mei woke him. She was sitting up. "It's strange," she said, "I keep thinking about the base—Quon, Jack, Wes, and everyone there—and I wish we could go back."

"There is no more base," Rex said.

"I know, but I miss it," Mei said. "I never thought I'd say that, but I miss the base. My memories of Quon and Jack are there."

"I know what you mean, but I think it's finally time to go home."

"I'm worried. How are you going to get away from the Russian military?"

"I don't know yet. How are you going to explain everything to your mother-in-law?"

"I don't know, but I know that this baby saved us." Mei buried her head in Rex's shoulder and rested there.

Rex thought about the crew on the base. The loss of the potential these scientists had to offer the scientific community was upsetting. Feng Feng was a top graduate of the Hong Kong University of Science and

Technology. His mission was to harness solar energy and design a safe way of beaming it back to Earth. Judith was from rural Kentucky and the eldest of five siblings. She attended MIT on an academic scholarship. She was on the verge of an enormous breakthrough in commercializing clean nuclear fusion with Rex. Dana was a fellow alumnus of the California Institute of Technology only a few class years behind Rex. Then he thought of Ed. Rex was distressed by the loss of everyone in general. With respect to Ed, though, he blamed him for his complicity with the military in bringing nuclear weapons to the moon. It was difficult for Rex to sleep with these thoughts stirring him up. He studied the metal ceiling and noted that most of the bolts were loose on the panels above him. He hoped that they would not fall down on them while they slept.

CHAPTER TWENTY-FOUR

REX AWOKE TO the familiar aroma of coffee wafting across the room. He sat up and saw Dr. Gali standing in the doorway, drinking coffee and talking to Mei. Rex rolled himself out of bed since he was more than ready for some bad space station coffee. He walked over to them and noticed that the lights were working again. He heard Mei thank the doctor for his help. Dr. Gali appeared to be on his way out. "I am glad you feel better, my dear," Dr. Gali said as he left without acknowledging Rex. The doctor's footsteps echoed in the hallway as he ascended the stairs.

Rex took the doctor's place in the doorway by Mei. "Are you okay?"

"Yes," Mei said. "Let's walk. I'm ready to get out of here."

Rex motioned for Mei to lead the way. "After you."

They ascended the stairs and stopped to peek in on the happenings in the lounge. The crewmembers were gathered in groups, presumably discussing all that had transpired the night before. Rex wanted to stop and talk to find out if there was any new information, but Mei pulled him back up the staircase until they reached the cafeteria level. The kitchen was open and hot food was available. Unfortunately, there was only kasha, water, and coffee. Even though the meal was not particularly appealing, Rex poured himself some coffee and took a bowl of the cereal anyway. He had not had much to eat since he arrived and he was grateful that the station crew even bothered to make extra food for the Moon-X personnel. Mei took a bowl of the cereal and some water. Rex and Mei joined Xiao and Li Ling who were sitting at a table in the corner.

Li Ling started sharing information immediately. "They aren't jamming communications anymore; but there are no more satellites, so we can't reach anyone."

Xiao nodded his head in agreement. He looked very haggard and tired.

"Did you get any sleep?" Mei asked him.

"No, I was up walking around the station to see what was going on," Xiao said before he took a bite of his kasha.

"Did you find out anything?" Rex asked.

"We don't know if we're at war or if we even have a home to return to." Xiao's face flushed and his eyes began to tear up.

He isn't doing well, Rex thought. "Let's just stick to what we know for sure," he said. "Li Ling says communications are down, so we don't know what's going on at home. At least we are safe on the station."

"We'll never get home now," said Li Ling.

Rex realized that the enormity of the situation was too much for some to bear, and that there was nothing to be learned from the others except to confirm that they were indeed in trouble. Rex reflected on the situation. Miraculously, they had survived the initial explosion and bombardment by moon rock fragments. The station likely had limited supplies. He wondered how the Russians would treat the Moon-X employees now. The longer they were up here together, the more tense things were likely to get. They needed to find a way to be useful and stay out of the path of the soldiers.

"I think we should ask to see the broken shuttle," he said.

Xiao looked up. "Why?"

"We might be able to fix it."

"We don't even know what's wrong with it," Xiao said.

"I wouldn't know the first thing about fixing a shuttle," Li Ling said.

"But you could help with the communications issue," Rex said.

"Sure, I'm in," Li Ling said, "if you can convince the commander."

"Why don't they fix their own shuttle?" Mei asked.

"The only Russian qualified up here to fix it is Sergei," Rex said.

"Well, they mucked things up," Xiao said, "they might as well let us give it a go."

Li Ling was skeptical. "Even if they let us, then what?"

"Then we go home," Rex said.

"What if we are better off up here?" Xiao asked.

Mei nudged Xiao. "Seriously, better off here with these killers?"

"Right," Rex said.

"Do we have any aeronautical engineers in our group?" Mei asked.

"Sergei can help," Rex said, "he designed the *Minerva*."

Li Ling scoffed. "All the same, I'd rather have one of ours working on it."

"One of ours?" Rex argued. "He's a scientist, like us."

"But he's Russian," Li Ling said.

"So? I'm sure he wants to get home as much as you do," Rex said.

"Look at what just happened," Xiao said. "They didn't care much for their own ships."

"Sergei didn't have anything to do with that," Rex said.

"He might have," Li Ling said.

"Come on, you know him," Rex said.

"Not really," Xiao said.

"And look what happened to the *Minerva*," Li Ling said, "and he worked on that."

"That wasn't his fault," Rex said.

"How do you know?" Li Ling said. "We still don't know what happened to that ship."

"I'm sure it didn't have anything to do with his design," Rex said.

"I'm glad you're sure, but I'm not," Li Ling said. "In any event, I'd rather we had our own expert working on the shuttle, if it's even reparable."

"I think Kong went to Ha Gong Da," Xiao said.

Rex was unfamiliar with all of the Chinese universities. "What's Ha Gong Da?"

Mei explained. "That's short for Harbin Institute of Technology. It's one of the best engineering schools in China."

Li Ling put her spoon down in her bowl. "Yes, they even design and launch their own satellites. Sounds like he's someone to talk to."

"He's sleeping in the lounge," Xiao said.

"Do you think he'll be agreeable?" Rex asked.

Xiao laughed.

Rex turned to Xiao. "What's so funny?"

"Kong can be very difficult," Xiao said.

"I see," Rex said.

"He's like a moody teenager," added Li Ling.

"Well, he is only twenty-two," Mei said.

"I knew he was young, but not *that* young," Xiao said.

"Impressive," Rex said.

"How about you and Xiao go talk to him and Mei and I can go freshen up? I heard there are extra blankets on the upper level. I'm thinking we can lift a blanket or two." Mei accepted Li Ling's invitation and left with her. Rex finished his cereal, even though he did not care much for it.

Rex and Xiao caught up on what they had witnessed the night before. Xiao was perplexed by the cause of such destruction, while Rex was sickened by his knowledge of the hidden weapons in the crater and on the base. As the cafeteria filled up with Russian soldiers, Rex thought it was a good time for him and Xiao to make their exit. He motioned to Xiao. They got up and Xiao grabbed a fresh cup of coffee for Kong on the way out.

They found Kong asleep in the lounge under a table. Xiao put his hand on his shoulder and tried to wake him. Kong rolled away in the other direction. "Let me try." Rex knelt and spoke loudly near Kong's ear. "Hey, we need to talk to you."

"Go away," Kong said.

"Come on, get up," Xiao said. "We have coffee for you."

"Gross," Kong said.

"It's all they had in the kitchen besides water," Xiao said.

Kong buried his head under his blanket.

Xiao sat down. "We need your help with something."

"Leave me alone," Kong said.

"If you ever want to get back home," Rex said, "you need to help us."

"We're all going to die," Kong muttered from under his blanket.

"Maybe you should listen to what we have to say before assuming things," Rex said.

"It's too late."

"We need your help to fix the shuttle so we can get home," Rex said.

"Impossible."

"You don't know until you try," Rex said.

Kong continued speaking from under his blanket. "I don't need to try. I know."

Xiao attempted to lift the blanket from Kong's face. Kong held the blanket tightly and thwarted Xiao's effort. "You don't know," Xiao said.

"I know."

"We might be able to fix the shuttle and get home," Rex said. "Don't you want to help us?"

Kong stuck his head out from under his blanket. "Even if you fixed this broken-down shuttle, there is no way to reenter the earth's atmosphere safely. The only viable point of reentry would land us in the ocean, and we'd all drown."

"There might be a way," Rex said.

"There isn't."

Rex could see there was no moving him. He tried a different strategy. "Okay, maybe there isn't. Where would you rather die? Up here or back on Earth?"

Kong did not answer.

"Well?" Rex asked.

Kong sat up. His hair was disheveled with some strands sticking up vertically. Rex recognized Kong as the young man who had helped to unload Jack's cargo on his last run. Rex only spoke to him a few times on the base. Their paths did not cross much. Rex thought about Kong's youth and realized how fortunate it was that Kong had gotten on the evacuation shuttle. Maybe all was not lost.

"I can't swim," Kong said.

"So?" Rex asked.

"I'd prefer not to drown," Kong said.

"Help us find a way not to, then," Rex said.

Kong wrapped his blanket around himself. "I thought you said you had coffee?" Xiao handed Kong the coffee and he took a sip. "Vile."

"You'd love the kasha, then," Xiao said.

"Disgusting. Is there any other food?"

"No," Xiao said, "but maybe you'd prefer to starve to death up here with the Russians."

"All right, talk," Kong said.

Rex explained what he knew about the shuttle and his plan to try to help fix it. Kong listened without saying much or asking any questions.

"We don't know if they'll even let us near the shuttle," Rex said, "but I think they'd consider it."

"Do we have to take them, too?" Kong asked.

"I imagine so," Rex said.

Kong was silent again. Xiao tried coaxing him again. "Come on, everyone wants to get home."

"Have you thought about what we're going back to?" Kong asked.

"Yes, and it doesn't matter," Xiao said.

"You know the tides could have shifted directions by now. There could be tsunamis and earthquakes. There might not be any rescue boats to fetch us."

"We can work on that," Rex said.

"Well that's your job, then," Kong said.

"Agreed."

"And I don't want any Russians helping," Kong said.

"Not even Sergei?" asked Rex.

"Especially him," Kong said.

"That might be difficult. The commander might not go along with it if no Russians are involved," Rex said.

"Does he know how to fix a fuel leak in space?" Kong asked.

"I'm not sure I follow," said Rex.

"Unless Sergei or someone else on this station knows how to fix a fuel leak in space," Kong said, "the commander must let us do the work."

"Is that what's wrong with it?" Xiao asked.

"Of course," Kong said.

"How do you know that?" Rex asked.

"I smelled ammonia when I got on the shuttle," Kong said. "I don't think the pilots noticed."

"Hydrazine?" Rex asked.

"Yes," Kong said.

"Didn't you say anything?" Xiao asked.

"No," Kong said. "I figured the leak would freeze up, and they wouldn't use the reaction control system for the trip to the station."

"Do they know about the leak?" Rex asked.

"I'm sure they figured it out when they saw they were losing fuel," Kong said.

"Why can't they fix it?" Rex asked.

Kong laughed. "You think the maintenance crew knows how to do anything without calling their engineers on the ground?"

"What about Sergei?" Rex asked.

"He can't do it alone," Kong said, "and the commander probably won't let him."

"I see," Rex said.

"They definitely need us to do it, then," Xiao said.

The three of them talked until Kong finished his coffee. Then Rex left to talk to the commander.

CHAPTER TWENTY-FIVE

AS REX ASCENDED the staircase, two soldiers walked down toward him. He recognized one of the men as the short soldier he had fought with on the moon. Rex looked down, trying not to make eye contact. He continued walking, hoping to pass the men quickly. Since there was not enough room for three to pass each other on the stairwell, one soldier slowed down and walked behind the other so they would have room to pass Rex. The first soldier passed by Rex without incident; but as the other soldier passed, he nudged Rex hard with his elbow, shoving him into the bulkhead. Rex almost lost his footing but saved himself by skipping a step. He heard the men say something in Russian and then laugh. Rex moved on. He knew he would not last long on the station if he started a fight after every offense, even though he wanted to pummel both of them.

Rex reached the third floor and saw that the commander's office door was open. When he got close enough, he heard the commander talking to someone. He waited for the soldier to leave before slipping inside. The commander was sitting at his desk.

The commander sat back in his chair as if surprised to see Rex. "What do you want? Have you reconsidered my offer?"

Rex tried to be as concise and contrite as possible. "Given recent developments, getting back to Earth is going to be difficult. I would like to try and repair the shuttle."

The commander tilted his head to the right, and then he stood up. "You would like to repair the shuttle?"

"Yes, along with some of the Moon-X crew."

"Do you even know what's wrong with it?" the commander asked.

"There's a hydrazine leak."

The commander walked around his desk and stood close to Rex in an intimidating manner. "How do you know that?"

"One of the Moon-X crewmembers smelled ammonia on the way up here," Rex said.

"And they said nothing?"

"He knew they wouldn't need to use the reaction control system."

The commander sat down on top his desk in front of Rex and looked down at him. "It is too dangerous to fix the leak near the station, and we have our own engineers."

"If you mean Sergei, he can't do it alone, and your men are busy right now running the station and keeping us afloat."

"You know the moon was destroyed last night," the commander said, "and this station almost went with it."

"Yes, how could I not?"

"That couldn't have happened unless there were nuclear weapons on the moon," the commander said. "Did you know there were weapons down there?"

"Just let us fix the shuttle."

"If I allow you to fix the shuttle," the commander asked, "what will you give me in return?"

"Getting your men back safely isn't enough?"

"No one is in a hurry to leave," the commander said.

"Not yet, but what about three months from now when your supplies start to run out?"

"There's no hurry," the commander said.

"Do you really think a ship will come?"

"Eventually."

"I'm sure the Chinese government would be most appreciative if you got their best and brightest home right now," Rex said.

"That's not my concern. Why didn't you tell me about the nuclear weapons before this happened?"

The commander's words stung. Rex questioned himself whether he could have stopped the attack by telling the commander about the weapons, but that would have been disloyal to the company and his country. He put these thoughts aside and tried to hide his discomfort.

"I don't know anything about that," Rex said, trying not to fidget in his seat.

"You seem to know quite a lot about what's going on up here."

"I only want to help."

"I believe I made you a job offer."

"You want me to accept?"

"Yes, accept the offer or tell me about the nuclear weapons. Those are your options."

"I don't know anything about weapons on the moon."

"Then accept the job offer."

"If I accept, will you let us work on the ship undisturbed?"

"Of course, as long as you do not put the station in danger."

"And you'll provide parts and supplies as needed?"

"As long as they are available."

Rex thought about the commander's terms. If he did not accept the job, the Russian military would take him. It was not as if they would let him go home. He thought for a moment about the scientists on the base. If he had told the commander about the nuclear weapons on the base, perhaps Feng Feng and the others would be alive.

The commander grew impatient and stood up again. "If you have nothing more to say, you can leave my office."

Rex got up and turned to leave but hesitated before exiting. The thought of anything happening to the remaining Moon-X crew while waiting for a rescue, knowing that he could have done something to get them home got to him.

Rex turned back around. "Okay, I accept your offer."

The commander smiled. "Yes?"

Rex nodded. "Yes."

"Good." The commander walked back around his desk and tapped a few buttons on the computer screen. "All I need from you is to sign this form." The commander manipulated the electronic document to face the other way and pushed it toward Rex's side of the desk.

Rex looked at the document on the desk screen and tried to read the first page. "It's in Russian."

"Of course, it's a Russian form," the commander said.

"What does it say?"

"It says that you accept a scientific position with the Russian Federation."

"What else does it say?"

"That's it," the commander said.

"It looks like a very long form."

"You know how Russian is. A lot of words to say one thing."

Rex did not trust the commander and he knew it was a bad idea, but he signed the form with his finger. As soon as he did, he knew that he should not have. He reassured himself that he could sort it all out when he got back to Earth. The commander's smile widened, and Rex's stomach dropped.

"One more thing," the commander said.

Rex looked up at the commander, already feeling his stomach churn. "What's that?"

"You'll need to let Sergei supervise the work."

"I thought we had a deal."

"We do, but you have to involve Sergei."

"Fine." Rex told himself that he would figure out way to integrate Sergei into their work just enough to keep everyone happy. The commander held out his hand. Rex begrudgingly shook it.

CHAPTER TWENTY-SIX

REX SEARCHED THE station to find Sergei. He went to Sergei's room, lab, the cafeteria, and even walked by the control room to try to find him by listening for his voice. The station was a mess from the night before. Rex nimbly avoided the exposed wiring and wreckage on the floor. With no sign of Sergei in any of the likely places where Rex thought he'd be, Rex decided to check out the sixth floor. He also thought it would be helpful to get a look at the shuttle docking area.

The sixth floor was dimly lit. Although electricity had been restored to most of the station, the corridor was still dark. Rex reasoned that this was likely due to this deck being a lower priority. The door to the docking bay was not locked, and Rex walked right in. The bay was large with a high ceiling and a window along the left side, and there were large metal storage containers randomly strewn about in the middle of it; they must have gotten knocked around when the station was jostled about, he reasoned. There was a passageway in each corner and several more large metal storage boxes around the perimeter of the room. Rex guessed that they contained equipment or food. Rex walked toward the window and spied Sergei sitting on a metal crate. He was gazing out the horizontal window, which had a view of the earth. Rex alerted him to his presence.

"I've been looking all over for you."

Sergei turned around. "You found me."

"I assume you got things under control last night."

"We survived."

"I think we have you to thank for that."

"Don't thank me. We survived by the skin of my teeth."

"We're still here," Rex said. "That's all that matters."

"Really? Have you looked out there? There's no moon!"

Rex could tell that Sergei was very worked up. "Have you slept?"

"Not yet. I can't."

"Have you had anything to eat?"

"I can't eat."

"How did you maneuver the station?"

"When I got to the command center, everyone was in a panic. They didn't know how to move the station. I started the thrusters, but I was only able to move the station in one direction—up." Sergei pointed with his finger for emphasis. "Eventually, I was able to steer us into an new orbit."

"Thank goodness you were there," Rex said.

"I just don't understand what happened."

"What do you mean?"

"I knew they were working on a directed energy weapon," Sergei said, "but no weapon could destroy something the size of the moon in one shot like that."

"Do you know what kind of energy weapon it was?" Rex asked.

"They kept everything so secret, like I told you, but last night the commander was talking. He said it was a neutral particle beam weapon."

"They were able to create one?"

"It seems so."

"What kind of atoms? Hydrogen?"

"Yes, using an RF-LINAC," Sergei said.

"A radio frequency linear accelerator?" Rex asked.

Sergei nodded.

"How did they power it?"

"With a high energy laser," Sergei said.

"Really? They used a laser to power the accelerator?"

"I thought it was clever, too," Sergei said.

"But you didn't know any of this before?"

"No, I just heard the details last night," Sergei said. "They were trying to figure out what went wrong."

"What kind of high energy laser was it?"

"A carbon dioxide gas dynamic laser. The GDL worked as a laser jet engine as well."

"That's a real accomplishment, but also an unfortunate one," Rex said.

"Yes, but even so, there's no way that the beam could have produced enough power to destroy the moon."

"Was the weapon tested before?"

"No."

"Maybe it was more powerful than they thought," Rex said.

"Not possible. It can heat up and destabilize the area that it targets, but the beam can only be sustained for a few seconds. At most, the affected area would be about the size of a large crater. Not a planet buster at all. The commander said that there must have been nuclear weapons hidden somewhere," Sergei said, looking up at Rex.

"Where did they fire it?"

"By Sverdrup Crater."

Rex's face grew pale; he understood exactly what had happened, but he couldn't tell anyone—not even Sergei.

"Are you okay? Do you know something?"

Rex wanted to confide in Sergei but held back. "I'm fine. It's just that Sverdrup Crater is where I hurt my knee."

"Yes, I know," Sergei said.

"Were all of the Russian ships destroyed in the explosion?"

"Yes," Sergei said.

"I see. Where is the broken shuttle?" Rex asked, looking around the docking bay.

Sergei pointed to the right corner. "Just down that corridor, you'll find the docking hatch."

"I was talking to a few of the scientists this morning. I was thinking that we could try to fix the shuttle."

Sergei shook his head. "You really think you can fix that up here? With no supplies?"

"It's worth a try."

"If we wait it out, someone will send a shuttle."

Rex leaned against the window. "With all that is going on, do you really think anyone is worried about us up here or that they could even get to us?"

"The commander is trying to make contact with the ground."

"Sure, but who could even launch with all the debris in the atmosphere? We don't even know how much damage they've sustained down there."

"Exactly, so how is the shuttle going to avoid the debris?" Sergei asked.

"It's easier to get down because we can descend from a safe position and land in multiple spots," Rex said. "Ships from Earth can only take off from areas that aren't affected by the debris."

"Supposing it's possible to fix it, where would you land?"

"The ground," Rex said.

Sergei shook his head. "The coasts were probably hit by tidal waves already. There won't be any country ready to receive us."

"Let's worry about the landing once we've gotten the shuttle working."

"Why are you doing this?" Sergei asked. "You know the military isn't going to let *you* go home."

"No, but I want to help what's left of the Moon-X crew get home," Rex said.

"Well, if you can convince him, I will help."

Rex paused. "I already spoke to him. He said we could go ahead, but he wants you involved."

"Really? Why didn't you say so?"

"I just did."

"I'll help, but I don't know if we can make the necessary repairs under these conditions."

Rex debated internally whether to bring up the fact that the others did not want to work with him. He decided to say something since it would be more awkward to bring up later.

"There's one more thing," Rex said.

"What's that?"

"Some of the crew would prefer that you not be involved."

"Why?"

"They're suspicious of all Russians now," Rex said, "and they brought up the *Minerva*."

"They blame *me*?"

"You know how it is. They're very afraid right now."

"Well, there's no way the commander will sign off without me being involved."

"Maybe you could be a hands-off advisor?"

"I have plenty to do around here, anyway. If the commander lets you go ahead, I'll be your silent advisor."

"He already did."

Sergei put his shoulders back, as if something had just occurred to him. He looked Rex directly in the eye. "How did you get the commander to agree to this?"

Rex was reluctant to tell him. He was embarrassed because he knew that he shouldn't have signed anything, but he had his reasons for going along with it. "I agreed to go to work for the Russian Federation."

"Are you crazy in the head?" Sergei said, slapping himself in the head.

"I had to agree. It was the only way to get his permission to fix the shuttle."

"You should have waited."

"How long can we wait? Nobody's coming, and you see how the soldiers look at us. It's only a matter of time until they start abusing us."

"The commander would never let that happen."

"I don't know. I just wanted to help."

"Did you sign anything?"

"Yes."

Sergei shook his head again. "You're throwing your life away."

"I'll figure something out."

"How?" Sergei asked in a demanding tone.

"I don't know."

Sergei stood up and walked to the window. He looked out and then back at Rex. "I might be able to help you, but you have to tell me something."

"What?"

"Were you working on weapons in your lab?"

"Are you kidding? Absolutely not." Rex was offended that Sergei would think that he would participate in a secret weapons program.

"Truth?"

"I swear."

"There must have been weapons on the base," Sergei said. "There is no weapon that could do that much damage without the help of nuclear detonations."

Rex wanted to tell Sergei what he knew, but he held back. "We'll never know for sure."

"But you know, don't you?"

"Why do you say that?" Rex's hands were sweating.

"Because you know things. You spent all of your time on the base gathering information about the *Minerva* and always bothering Ed for more information on every little happening. Nothing happened on that base without your knowledge."

Rex took a deep breath but said nothing.

"I know you know something," Sergei said.

"Sergei, don't do this."

"What are you not telling me?"

"Sergei, please."

"I told you what I found out about the *Minerva*. Tell me what happened to the base."

"That weapon destroyed the moon!"

Sergei persisted. "It's not possible and you know it."

"How can you say that if you don't know how powerful that weapon was?"

"Rex, either you tell me what you know or I won't help you."

"I can't," Rex said, realizing that he made an inadvertent admission.

"So you *do* know something."

Rex stood up. "If I knew anything, it would be considered a government secret."

"I told you what happened to the *Minerva*."

"That's different."

"How?"

"You have a different relationship with your government," Rex said.

"Right. My government will kill me if they find out I shared any information with you about the *Minerva*. Yours will only put you in jail."

"I don't know anything."

"Now you lie."

"I would be a traitor if I said anything."

Sergei moved closer to Rex in a manner that would have been perceived as aggressive if Rex did not know Sergei better. "You are a traitor. You signed a letter agreeing to work for the Russian Federation."

Rex moved away from Sergei and closer to the window. "There is no more fusion work. The helium-3 is gone. The world is probably in complete chaos; fusion is the last thing anyone is going to care about."

"And what about you?" Sergei asked. "Are you ready to give up your life's work?"

"I want to get Mei and the other scientists home safely," Rex said.

"Right. So tell me what the bloody hell happened."

Rex looked away, internally debating what to do.

"You think I agree with everything my government does?" Sergei asked.

"No," Rex said.

"I cannot change my government, but I can decide for myself what is right and wrong."

"There's nothing I can say."

"If I am going to help you," Sergei said. "I need to know that you are not keeping secrets from me."

"I understand."

"Spill it, Rex, and I will make that letter go away."

"How?"

"I will retrieve it. The commander is disciplined and calculating, but he is not a good housekeeper."

"You can you get rid of it?"

"With your help," Sergei said.

Rex knew signing that letter had been a mistake. If he could take it back now, he would. The trade-off for fixing his mistake was potentially worse if Sergei betrayed him. Sergei had never lied to him, but he never had a reason to. For a moment Rex considered that Sergei might be trying to trick him into revealing military secrets for the commander. However, he had never known Sergei to be chummy with the military types.

"I can't say anything more," Rex said, "but I know you mean well."

"Think about it, then. If you decide you have something to tell me, meet me up here early tomorrow morning. I want to help you, but I need to know the truth."

Rex thanked Sergei and left, walking down the stairs toward the lounge.

※

Rex interrupted a conversation between Xiao and Kong to tell them that he had gotten the commander's permission to fix the shuttle.

"How'd you get him to agree to that?" Xiao asked.

"I sold my soul," Rex said.

"I'll bet," Xiao said.

"When do we get started?" Kong asked.

"We have nothing else to do," Rex said, "let's get to it."

"Wait," Xiao said, "let's discuss our strategy here."

"What do you mean?" Rex asked.

"I mean how are we going to approach this repair?" Xiao asked. "What about the water landing? What are our options to repair the RCS?"

Kong grinned. "Just leave it to me."

"I plan to, Kong," Xiao said, "but we need to work out some of these details."

"I propose we inspect the shuttle first," Rex said.

"Shouldn't we wait for Mei and Li Ling?"

"We'll fill them in and they can get started with us tomorrow," Rex said.

The three of them walked up to the sixth floor that was now empty and made their way to the entrance to the shuttle's dock in the far right-hand corner of the room. The key code on the door was in Russian, but Kong was able to open it. They stepped inside.

The interior of the shuttle was nothing like Rex remembered, but his memory of the ship was limited to the brief few seconds that he was conscious on it. They spread out and each made their own assessment of the interior. They regrouped in the middle seating area, which was a converted cargo module.

Rex turned to Xiao. "What do you think?"

"We need to fix the leak," Xiao said. "This is a pretty makeshift craft. Their modifications have probably weakened the hull."

"We will need to drain the fuel tank to fix it," Kong said.

"We'll need permission for that," Rex said. "Why don't we figure out our repair plan first? I don't want to go back to the commander to ask for anything unless we absolutely have no choice."

"All right," Kong said.

"Where do we start?" Rex asked.

"Let's ignite this firecracker and see how she runs," said Kong.

They walked back to the flight deck and sat down in front of the controls. Kong took the lead, as he could read Russian. He sat down by the control panel and turned on the electricity to test the ion engine.

"Do you think we need some help from a Russian engineer?" Rex asked. He hoped this was his opportunity to get support for bringing in Sergei's help.

Kong swung his chair around. "No. Why?"

"The controls are all in Russian," Rex said.

"Doesn't bother me," Kong said.

"Yes, but you can't do everything alone," Xiao said.

"I think we should reconsider Sergei's help," Rex said.

"He might be able to help," Xiao said.

Kong rolled his eyes and pointed at a lever under the computer screen. "We're scientists. Look at this logically. What do you think that button is for?"

Rex took a closer look. "Communications?"

"No," Kong asked. "What do you think, Xiao?"

Xiao stood up to take a closer look. "Thrusters?"

"No," Kong said. "You two aren't right for this job. Maybe some of the others could help."

"I don't think you'll find the others any more helpful," Xiao said. "Nobody else up here speaks Russian."

Kong relented. "Bring Sergei up here and have him show everyone around the controls."

Rex was glad that Sergei would be able to help them repair the shuttle. He trusted Kong's expertise, but he knew they needed a Russian intermediary for many reasons, translation being only one; the commander's directive, another.

"How are we going to drain the hydrazine?" Xiao asked.

"Why don't we think about it and meet up here tomorrow morning?" Rex suggested.

"And I'll talk to the crew and see who else wants to help," Xiao said.

They finished inspecting the shuttle and then returned to the lounge to strategize.

CHAPTER TWENTY-SEVEN

MOST OF THE crew was sleeping; but Rex walked around the room, inspecting the damage done to the lounge. The Moon-X crew cleared the broken tables away from their sleeping area, but they left the large metal beam lying in the middle of the room, and several broken chairs and tables were still strewn about the lounge. A few people were still up talking. Rex stopped to take in the view from the lounge window, which now displayed the South Pole. The field of moon rock debris had massed together to form a large, expansive ring around the earth's equator. The sight was both amazing and horrifying. The earth was transformed in a single night into a planet with a ring.

Mei caught up to Rex. She dropped both of their bags on the floor by Rex's feet. "I brought some of your stuff down from Sergei's room."

"Thanks," Rex said, "but there's actually nothing useful in there."

"I know," Mei said, "that's why I stuffed it with some clean clothes and blankets from the crew's laundry."

"Good thinking. How's your wrist?"

"It's all right."

They looked out the window. Rex put his arm around Mei. "It looks like a different planet, doesn't it?"

"I wonder what's going on down there. Do you think there were tidal waves and earthquakes?"

"Yes, but I don't know how strong or where."

"I hope that's the worst of it."

"What do you mean?"

"There could be nuclear reactor leaks," Mei said, "not to mention all the new issues around the planet due to communications being disabled by nonfunctioning satellites."

"Maybe it stopped a war."

"Or started one."

"What do you think the governments are doing?"

"Hopefully they are taking care of their people."

"Somehow I think they are in self-preservation mode."

Mei sat down pulled out the blankets from her bag and handed one to Rex. "Aren't we all?"

Rex sat down next to Mei and spread out the blanket. "I suppose," he said as he stretched out onto the blanket.

Mei lay down next to him. "Are you tired?"

"Yes, but I can't sleep. I used to enjoy your Jade rabbit tales."

"He's gone now."

"We'll have to imagine him living among the broken bits."

"No."

"Why not?"

"That's depressing," Mei said.

"Maybe he hopped to the stars. Let's look for him there, then."

"We'll have to make up a whole new story for him."

"Yes, how he leapt from the moon to the stars. That sounds better, doesn't it?"

"Yes. Let's look in the constellation Lepus."

"Can you see it from here?"

"Look there." Mei pointed out Orion's belt since that would make finding Lepus easier. Mei abruptly sat up. "Oh, no."

"What is it?"

Mei pointed back to the earth, at a plume of black smoke emanating from the area near the border of Chile and Argentina. "That must be Copahue," she said.

"It's erupting." Rex pointed to another plume. "And over there." He pointed at the smaller plume coming from the southern tip of Australia. "I'm not sure which one that is, maybe Mount Gambier."

"It's happening everywhere," Mei said.

"I only see two."

"That's all we can see from up here. The tsunamis probably already hit. The earth's axis could even be affected." Mei got up and moved closer to the window. Rex followed. He knew that her suppositions were all real possibilities. He did not want any of them to be true; but he saw more plumes, which meant that Mei was probably correct that there were more eruptions happening all over the planet.

"I can't believe we're standing here," Rex said. He thought of Feng Feng, Dana, Judith, Ed, and Wes.

Mei intuitively knew what Rex was thinking. "They're all gone. Everyone we ever knew up here."

"Except us evacuees," Rex said.

"How did this happen? What in the world could do *that* to the moon?"

As much as Rex wanted to, he knew he could not discuss the nuclear weapons with Mei yet. If he had not fought with Ed that night, he could have had the satisfaction of blaming the Russians for all of the destruction, but he knew the truth. He answered as honestly as he could. "Human foible."

"We could have done so much better," Mei said.

Rex nodded.

"You know, I was ambivalent about the baby. I thought I could go on as normal for as long as possible and avoid acknowledging it—avoid all the problems—but I *want* a baby. I want a family now. I didn't know it before, and now there's probably nothing but disaster to go home to—if we can even get there."

"Whatever is going on down there, it will be all right," Rex said. "You and the baby will be all right."

Mei clutched Rex's arm. "Is this the end of the world?"

"No. It's the beginning of a new world—a new era."

"I think it's time we stopped telling each other fairy tales," Mei said.

"What would you have us do?"

"Face the facts. We may never get home and if we do we may not like what we find."

"It will be okay—it has to be."

"How can you be all right with all of this?"

"I'm not. My world already ended; and somehow I'm still here, still breathing."

"But things are getting worse, not better."

"Mei, every loss is its own apocalypse. I don't know what's going to happen, but it doesn't matter. We have to go on because we're still here, and it's not up to us when it's over. There were times that I wished I had been on the *Minerva*, but I wasn't. I can't change what happened, but if I give up, I know that nothing she or I wanted will ever happen; and that's what's tragic—unfulfilled potentiality."

Rex took Mei by the hand and led her back to the blankets. He shared Mei's concerns. He was sickened by what happened to Wes, and the base, and the moon, and now the earth. Mei and Rex sat together watching the earth, the debris field, and the streaming plumes of volcanic smoke for a long time before turning away. It was as if the universe was unraveling before them. Rex wished that he could leap from the station and land safely back on Earth and find out that all was well; but the laws of physics were against him, as was the reality he was now facing. After tossing and turning a good while, Rex determined that there must be a way to set things right. If science had brought forth the destruction, then science could fix it. All he needed to do was to get home.

TO BE CONTINUED